WOULD IT BE OKAY TO LOVE YOU?

Year Two

AMY TASUKADA

ACKNOWLEDGEMENTS

THANK YOU TO THE awesome people that read the book at various drafts, Nell Iris, and Addison Albright. Finally, you. Thanks for giving my book a chance!

OCTOBER

AOI RUBBED BEHIND HIS ears, but the moment he stopped, the ache from the bunny-ears headband returned. He shifted his weight to the other foot, hoping his discomfort didn't show on his face. He could deal with the pain to keep up the lighthearted mood of the Halloween script he was reading.

Three other voice actors dotted the stage, each with a microphone in front of them and a script in their hands. They were all bigger names than Aoi, but the moment Aoi had slipped on the ears to match his character, he'd become the audience favorite.

"We're getting far away from the others," Aoi read.

"That's because the surprise is just for you."

"Oh…" Aoi lifted the tone, the higher pitch invoking a yen for something more his character had been wishing for since the beginning of the piece.

The fluffy storyline meant Aoi couldn't show off his moaning talents, but it was nice to take a break from the more erotic stories. Besides, he was playing a young high school student who spent most of the time not realizing he'd been flirted with. It reminded Aoi too much of his first date with Sato, his boyfriend.

"You didn't have to go through all the trouble," Aoi read.

"But I wanted to. I hope you'll like it."

Aoi ran his finger over the edge of the worn script pages. He'd marked them up with little doodles and notes to himself. He followed along as the three others who shared the stage said their lines. Then his cue came.

Aoi read aloud the internal monologue. "The door opened, and inside was a wonderful feast. Even in the scary castle, the food presented before me was the most beautiful thing I'd ever seen. Well, it was until I looked into Hitoshi's eyes. The same tingling feeling covered my whole body. I wanted to leave, but then I was caught in his gaze, and when our lips met, the rest of the world disappeared. I knew this was meant to be."

The audience applauded, and all the actors joined hands and bowed. The applause faded when the host came back onstage.

"We have a few minutes for questions. If you could just line up at the microphone, we'll get through as many as we can."

A stagehand brought stools out for the actors. Aoi adjusted his to the highest setting, hoping to at least do a decent job of making himself appear as tall as the other actors. He frowned as his legs dangled above the metal bar for his feet. The audience chuckled, and Aoi laughed along with them. The world wasn't built for people less than five feet tall.

The first woman in line took the microphone. "Hi. I was wondering what everyone's favorite snack was?"

"I really like dried squid," Aoi said.

The other actors rattled off their responses while Aoi gazed out at the audience. The bright lights blinded him from seeing the first few rows of people, but he could make out the faces toward the back. He took a second to smile at each one, but then his eyes grew wide.

Sato sat in the back corner.

He'd never come to any of Aoi's live events.

It wasn't like Sato wasn't supportive, but no men ever came to the events. He shouldn't have risked being spotted. It would be catastrophic if some fan figured out he and Sato were dating. It was one thing to voice-act gay characters but another thing to actually be gay. His career would be tossed away like bad dialogue.

Aoi bit his lip, and each of the faces he'd smiled at moments before pierced him with their knowing gazes. He gulped, but his mouth remained dry.

Sato had become so much bolder with their relationship after he'd come out to his parents. He would walk next to Aoi a little closer, and their hands would accidentally brush against each other more often in large crowds. If they ever managed to snag a train seat, Sato would scoot so close he might as well be on Aoi's lap. Coming to a reading was too much, too dangerous.

Aoi jiggled his foot. There were a lot of people here, so maybe a few men had been dragged along by their girlfriends. It might be okay. If anyone got suspicious, Sato could pretend the girl next to him was his date—if he didn't blurt out he was dating one of the actors onstage. Aoi mentally groaned. Why couldn't he have waited at a nearby café like he'd always done?

"Aoi?" the host asked.

Aoi jumped, and the audience laughed. "Sorry."

"So what is it? I'm sure all the ladies are dying to hear your answer?"

Acid churned in his stomach, and he let out a hesitant laugh. "What was the question again?"

Not only did the audience laugh, but so did the other voice actors. The woman at the microphone cleared her throat and tugged on her ponytail.

"I asked what *you* looked for in a girlfriend."

"Just me?"

Another chuckle from the audience—at least they found his floundering funny.

"I—ah." Aoi closed his eyes and pressed the bunny-ears headband tighter into his scalp.

"Everyone's on the edge of their seats for the answer," the host said.

"I guess I want a girlfriend who can cook meals with me. Maybe athletic so she can keep up when I train for marathons. Someone shorter than me would be nice, but that's probably impossible."

He'd described everything Sato wasn't. It would throw off anyone who'd had even an inkling that he and the adorable man with the dark-rimmed glasses in the back could possibly be together—if he were to ever admit he was gay, that was, which he would never do anyway.

A few more questions were asked but none as dangerous. During each one, Aoi tried not to stare at Sato, but his gaze couldn't help but end up there. The burning flood in his stomach rose to the back of his throat. He needed to get out of there.

The host finally called the event to a close, and Aoi followed his costars to the dressing rooms.

He pulled off the bunny ears and brushed aside his fan gifts the stagehand had placed on a chair. He plopped down. Ignoring the other actors as they chatted and opened their gifts, Aoi pulled out his phone.

Meet me out back in a half hour, Aoi texted Sato.

You were awesome, Sato replied.

We need to talk. Aoi let it sit in the loading screen before hitting Send.

He put away the phone, not wanting to see Sato's response, then slouched in the chair.

Usually, Aoi enjoyed reading the fan notes and chatting with his costars backstage while the fans left, but even glancing at his bag of gifts made him want to vomit. Each letter was another person who would reject everything Aoi had ever acted in if they found out he was gay.

Aoi didn't know how long he'd stared at the spot on the wall across the room, but eventually, management gave them the all clear to leave. He swallowed and waited for the others to leave before he moved. If they saw him and Sato meeting up, they'd know too.

How could Sato be so careless?

The back door slammed shut behind Aoi, and numbness crept from his feet to his body. He couldn't move. He could only stare at Sato as he leaned against the wall.

"You were awesome!" Sato said.

Aoi gave a faint smile. "There were a few parts I wish I'd done better with."

"No, you were perfect. Everyone loved it. Especially the ears."

The ache behind Aoi's ears flared up again. He'd wear the stupid headband the rest of his life if he didn't have to worry about Sato showing up and possibly outing him again.

Aoi stuffed his hands into his pants pockets. How was he supposed to tell his boyfriend he didn't want to see him? The rough denim of his jeans scratched at Aoi's thumb with each stroke.

"I was a bit shocked to see you there," Aoi said.

"I've been stuck at the office so much lately I wanted to surprise you. With the bigger crowd, I thought I wouldn't stick out."

Aoi frowned. "I get wanting to come, but…"

"But what?"

A sweet smile filled Sato's face, and usually, it could melt any of Aoi's worries, but he couldn't get lost in Sato's smile today.

Aoi swallowed and looked away. "When I saw you, it made me nervous."

"Oh, I'm sorry. I didn't know it would be harder for you to act."

"What if someone found out?"

Sato pushed up his glasses. "I don't think—"

"Everyone could see. They might figure out I'm gay, and then I'm stuck without a job."

"No one would make the assumption—"

Aki shook his head. "You don't understand."

"I only wanted to come because I could only hear your performances on CD before. I wanted to see you act live once."

"You might be ready, but I'm not. I can't see you in the audience ever again."

Sato's mouth dropped, and Aoi's eyes widened. Not at Sato but at the woman with the ponytail. She rounded the corner and approached without hesitation.

"I see you did read my note about meeting out back after the show," she said.

"Actually, I didn't read…"

She brushed passed Sato, and Aoi took a step back.

"I know a wonderful café nearby. You can see if I match your ideal girl."

Sato cleared his throat and slid between them. Aoi's heart thumped against his ribs. Sato wouldn't be bold enough to say what Aoi thought he would.

"I'm sorry, miss," Sato said, "but Mr. Aoi has a very busy schedule to keep."

She frowned and leaned around Sato. "I was asking Aoi, not you."

Damn fangirls were getting pushier by the day. Sato took a step to the side to block her view.

"As Mr. Aoi's manager, I think I know better." He crossed his arms. "Please leave, or else I'll be forced to call security."

"Fine. You have my number, so call me if you ever want to go running." She winked before turning on her heel.

Aoi's heart echoed in his ears until she was out of sight.

Sato's hand hovered over Aoi's shoulder. He wouldn't touch him in public, not after what Aoi had said. Aoi smiled. Sato was too sweet for his own good sometimes.

No wonder Aoi had fallen in love with him.

"You okay?" Sato asked.

"As long as we don't run into any more."

Sato pushed up his glasses and gave a dorky smile. "Then I'll pretend to be Mr. Sato, head manager to Mr. Aoi. Should I come to all of your events?"

Aoi laughed. "No more surprise visits."

"Then how about we head home and cook dinner together."

"That's exactly what I want in a boyfriend."

NOVEMBER

A CHILL ROLLED ACROSS Sato's hips even though he was under a blanket. He groaned, still half-asleep, and tried to pull the cover closer, but a heavy weight prevented it from moving.

"Sato," Aoi almost sang.

Sato rubbed his eyes and looked up to his blurry blond boyfriend straddling his hips. Aoi still wore his blue athletic shorts from his morning run, and he had a crooked smile on his face. He wiggled his ass against Sato's hips, making his cock twitch. If Aoi wanted weekend morning sex, it would be easier without the cloth separating them. Sato's fingers trailed down Aoi's exposed thigh, but he drew them back.

"Why are you so cold?" Sato asked.

"It's snowing outside."

"But it's only November."

"For like two more days."

"It's still too early. That means winter will be horrible this year."

Aoi stuck out his tongue and grinded more. "It's never as bad as you make it out to be. Come on. It's snowing!"

If all the wiggling was for Aoi to pretend to be a meteorologist and not for sex, then Sato was going back to sleep. It was too early for anything else. He yawned and tried to ignore his twitching length.

Aoi finally came to his senses that five in the morning was not the time to spell out the wonders of snow and slid off. But Aoi didn't crawl under the covers with him or head to the bath. Instead he grabbed the blanket Sato had cocooned himself in and tugged at the edge.

"What are you doing?" Sato mumbled.

"Let's go outside."

"But we don't have to go outside to snuggle."

Sometimes Aoi could make Sato's blood boil with a single seductive glance, but tugging on the covers was as attractive as the office during tax season. It was too early and too cold to go on some snow-filled fantasy. Especially since they'd stayed up late watching an old *Gundam* series. Then Aoi had distracted him with other things…

"I want to see the first snow with you," Aoi said.

Sato groaned and tried to turn over, but Aoi kept his grip on the blanket. He wasn't going to drop the snow fantasy adventure with Sato, was he?

"I'll get up after you're done with your bath," Sato said.

"But I don't need to take a bath. When I saw the snow, I decided not to run because I wanted to see it with you. It'll melt if we wait any longer."

"Maybe it'll snow later."

"Sato!"

"Fine."

Sato rubbed his eyes and groaned, but really, he'd do anything Aoi wanted. Even the blurry image of him made Sato's heart beat a little faster. He reached out and squeezed Aoi's hand. Each day with him only made him more excited about their life together. Aoi gave a final squeeze to Sato's hand and handed him his glasses. Sato slid them on, and Aoi came into focus. His smile looked more mischievous than before.

Aoi threw back the blanket, and goose bumps prickled Sato's skin. "See, you're already half-up now."

Sato groped desperately for the blanket, but it was gone. "How can you walk around in those shorts and not be freezing?"

"Come on. It'll all melt if we don't hurry up."

"Not everyone's used to waking before the sun."

Sato scooted off the bed and toward his closet. Each step sent a dull ache through him from the night before, but he tried not to show it. Yet after a few steps, he couldn't help but wince.

"You okay?" Aoi took Sato's hand and gave it a squeeze. "Was I too rough?"

Sato bent down and answered Aoi with a kiss. Kissing was always easier if they were both sitting since Aoi was so short, but sometimes Sato liked to emphasize the one advantage he had over his boyfriend.

"You did exactly what I wanted," Sato hummed into Aoi's ear.

"Always happy to satisfy."

Sato trailed his hand down Aoi's spine and rested it above his ass. Aoi let out a delicious moan, but of course he did since he moaned for a living. Yet the ones he gave Sato were always a little different from the ones in Aoi's boys' love drama CDs. Sato ran his hand over the silky nylon shorts then lightly pinched Aoi's butt.

"Hey!" Aoi laughed.

"You need to change out of those shorts if we're spending the day in snow."

"It's not *that* cold outside."

"Then I get to pinch those sweet cheeks of yours every time I see them." Sato gave another pinch for good measure.

"I see how it is."

Sato slid on a pair of black trousers and buttoned his dress shirt as Aoi rocked his hips and hummed a sexy tune.

"What are you doing?" Sato asked.

Aoi peeled off his shirt and tossed it at Sato. "Putting on a show?"

"Weren't you worried about the snow melting three seconds ago?"

Aoi shimmied his hips to one side, adding a dramatic drumroll sound with his tongue as he slipped the running shorts down. He knew how to tease every ounce of desire in Sato. Still, Sato had learned a thing or two about pleasing Aoi during their nearly two-year relationship.

Aoi finished getting dressed. His tight jeans and black shirt hugged his body. He slipped on the same too-thin-for-a-Tokyo-winter white jacket that he'd worn when they met. Sato bit his lip. It was the first snow of the year, so Aoi would probably be warm enough, but still. Sato pulled out the blue scarf he'd bought Aoi last Christmas and wrapped it around his neck.

"I'm going to burn up with all these layers," Aoi mumbled.

"You'll be fine."

"Let me get something real quick." He disappeared into in the kitchen then bounced back to Sato's side. "Okay, we can go."

They ventured into the cold and strolled to a nearby park. A light dusting of snow covered the leafy trees and street signs. Even though it had stopped snowing, there was something magical about seeing the world covered in white. The few people they passed wore smiles, and Sato had to admit his cheeks hurt from his own smile. Even the air he breathed smelled crisp and more alive.

"See? Isn't it pretty?" Aoi asked.

"It's nice."

It would've been nicer if Sato could reach out and interlace his fingers with Aoi's along their stroll, but the public display would've gotten a few prudish looks even if they were a straight couple. Since they were both men, it would be out of the question. Still, Sato stepped a little closer, and the few "accidental" brushes here and there sent little flutters of joy through Sato's body.

For Sato, coming out to his parents had been freeing, but since then, Aoi had been a bit more cautious about their proximity in public, especially around anime stores and after his live events. Even though Sato's parents hadn't welcomed the news with open arms, he knew in time they would see how much Aoi meant to him. Sato wanted both his parents and Aoi to be involved in his life.

Another accidental brush, and Aoi's short legs jumped a few steps ahead. His fans would love it if Aoi came out. They'd probably flock to everything he did more than if they continued thinking he was straight, but it wasn't Sato's place to bring it up.

"Thanks for waking me up," Sato said.

Aoi glanced back. "I knew you'd like it."

"Should we walk around the park a few times?"

"Nope."

"What?"

"I have something planned."

Sato pushed up his glasses. "Are you going to tell me this plan?"

"It's a secret."

"Aoi the PSIA agent."

Aoi laughed. "I don't think I'd pass the height requirement."

"But if they let you in, then no one would suspect it."

A few children played in the distance, their giggles carrying over the quiet morning. They walked past them and dodged a few other couples strolling along the same path.

"This looks perfect." Aoi stopped at a clear patch of undisturbed snow with no one else in sight.

"I can't disagree with Agent Aoi's keen observation."

"It's all elementary."

Sato laughed. "I think that's more a detective saying."

"Oh? What do spies say?"

"This meeting never happened?"

Aoi frowned. "I don't want to be a PSIA agent anymore."

The sun rose higher in the sky, and the few birds chirped their welcome. Aoi squatted and brushed together a clump of snow. There couldn't have been more than a centimeter of snowfall, so it took a lot to make a handful. Sato kneeled and made the same little bun out of the damp snow that Aoi had.

"Move it closer to mine," Aoi said.

The snow grew wet in Sato's hand, and the sun didn't help either. The consistency reminded Sato of the shaved ice he and Aoi had split during the summer. Aoi had eaten the mochi topping but had given most of the sweet red beans to Sato. They would have to do it again when shaved ice was back in season.

They pushed their oval buns of snow next to each other.

"Perfect," Aoi said.

"Yes, we made little igloos for bugs."

Aoi pulled out a baggie with red berries inside and placed one toward the front of one of the mounds. "They're not igloos."

Aoi placed another berry beside the first.

"I see now."

Sato stood. His legs were still a little stiff from the night's sleep, or maybe it was from the lack of sleep. In two strides, he found a group of fallen leaves and plucked them from the snow.

"There we go." Sato poked the leaves into the top of the small mounds and turned them into red-eyed rabbits.

"Your bunny's ears are kind of mismatched."

Sato stuck the taller leaf down a little more. "There we go. It's a little snow bunny family."

"Maybe they're two boyfriend bunnies."

Aoi shoved the ears of his bunny down so they were little points, and Sato's heart melted like the snow. It was them. Aoi's bunny had short ears, and his were kept long. Even though they couldn't always walk side by side, their bunnies could for as long as they lived.

Sato took off his glasses and rubbed his eyes. Shit. He was getting emotional about half-melted snow with fruit and leaves stuck into it.

"Two boyfriend bunnies still make a family," Sato said.

Aoi smiled. "You're right. They do."

DECEMBER

MICHIKO'S HUGS ALWAYS LEFT Aoi's stomach tight like when the mailman shoved one too many scripts into the mailbox.

Even in the dead of winter, Michiko's floral coat and cherry-blossom tights brought in a feeling of a warm spring breeze. Aoi pulled away from the embrace, but Michiko gave one last tight squeeze before letting go.

"I listened to *My Master's Wish* again on the train ride here," she squealed.

"I can't believe how popular that series got." Aoi rubbed his temple.

"It's because you were so good!"

Aoi gave a weary smile and backed away in case Michiko thought he deserved another hug for his voice-acting skills. The fact that Sato's sister actually liked him was hard enough to believe, but the fact she enjoyed the most scandalous drama he'd acted in was impossible. Aoi half expected she'd say, "Got ya," one of these days and turn into the rest of Sato's family and blame him for making their son gay.

Michiko changed out of her heels and into the slippers he offered, but even then, she stood a head above Aoi. He tugged down the sleeve of his sweater and stood a little straighter. Sato had to have come from a line of giants somewhere and never told him.

"Any insider knowledge on if there's going to be a sequel to *My Master's Wish*?" she asked.

Aoi laughed. "I hope not."

"But you and Atsushi had such chemistry."

"Just between us, there's a bigger chance of me acting in a straight drama CD than me getting along with Atsushi."

"Really? But he looks so cool. And that deep voice. Ah, I love hearing it—"

"He's an asshole."

"Oh…"

"Don't tell anyone I said that either." Aoi sighed. "He's so popular with directors. One bad word from him, and I'd be stuck doing commercials again."

"It's safe with me." She smiled.

Aoi plopped down in front of the kotatsu table with over a dozen scripts strewn over it. Michiko followed, sitting across from him.

"You said you wanted my help with something?" Michiko asked.

Aoi motioned to the scripts. All of them were high-lighted, and most had Aoi's drawings along the margins. He had read some of them at least a dozen times already, but when it came time to make a decision, his thoughts froze, unable to pick the right move for his career. It had been easier before *My Master's Wish* had become a hit. Before, he'd only received a script or two a month, but now, every day, a trip to the mailbox was like a trip to the boys' love section of an anime store.

"I can't decide which one to go for," Aoi said.

"Can't you do them all?"

"Some of them aren't as good as others, and a lot have overlapping recording schedules."

Michiko's eyes grew wide as she gazed at all the scripts. "All of these are going to get a release?"

"In a year or so."

"They're going to turn *A Single Night* into a movie!"

She grabbed the script and read through a few pages. She snatched another up and hugged it before doing the same. It was like he no longer existed.

Aoi stretched his legs, getting the full warmth of the heater underneath the table. Maybe it had been a bad idea to call Michiko. She would fangirl over each title like Sato did when a new Gundam model kit was announced.

Sato had been dropping too many hints about how Michiko knew a lot about boys' love and would be better at helping Aoi choose than him. Aoi had resisted for days, but when Sato had said it while adjusting his glasses, only to make them more askew, it had melted all of Aoi's defenses.

"I'll go make tea while you look over them," Aoi said, knowing it was better to allow Michiko's fangirl high lower naturally than try to force her to focus.

When Aoi returned from making tea, Michiko was stretched out on the floor, holding one of scripts above her head. The sunflower clip in her hair was crushed enough to resemble a Venus fly trap. He considered himself a fan of the boys' love genre too, but Michiko was something else.

She sighed happily. "It's like choose-your-own porn."

Aoi stared at her then cleared his throat. "The tea's ready."

He placed the mug on the table, and Michiko sat up, her hair clip once again the bright sunflower.

"Since you know what the fans like, I hoped you could point me in the right direction," Aoi said.

"I'd love to." Michiko took a sip of tea. "You know, I never expected Sato to date someone famous."

"I'm not famous."

"Well, to be honest, I never really expected Sato to date."

"Hey!"

Michiko glanced over the top of the script and shrugged. "He's nice and all, but you know he's one of the biggest dorks out there when it comes to robots. I never thought he'd be able to find someone who could put up with it."

"He's the sweetest guy I ever dated, and we all have our own hobbies."

Aoi couldn't say that Sato had probably learned how to be a dorky fan from his big sister. Maybe he would say it after Michiko told him what piece to act in.

"You even taught him to cook. When Mom gets over Sato being gay, she'll be impressed by you." Michiko took another sip of her tea.

His own tea grew too hot in his hand, and he felt his whole face flush. He put the cup down but didn't say anything.

She smiled. "I'm glad he met you."

"Me too," Aoi said, but it came out as more of a whisper than he'd intended.

Then Michiko gasped. Her eyes grew wide as she snatched the thickest script of them all. "They're making a dating simulation game based on *Nephilim Boys' School!*"

Aoi rubbed his ear, blocking the ringing after Michiko's squeal.

"Are dating sims popular among fans?" he asked.

"Are you kidding me? People obsess over them."

She hugged the paper and started to rock back and forth. "I can't wait to play it. The fan fiction for *Nephilim* is so awesome, but if there's a dating sim, then it'll get even hotter."

"But wouldn't fans get upset that my character ends up sleeping with all five guys?"

"You're going to play Hiroto? He's so adorable, Aoi. He's my favorite submissive ever, and to finally hear his moans…" She let out a dreamy sigh. "And yours are so heavenly."

Michiko pushed the conversation into a whole new state of awkward. If only her parents had an ounce of the same enthusiasm. Aoi cleared his throat, but Michiko still had the far-off look in her eyes.

"So people don't mind if my character sleeps with everyone?" Aoi asked.

"Haven't you played a dating sim game before?"

"Not really. I like reading manga more."

Michiko explained how dating sims worked with the player controlling a character and how the player's choices affected the outcome. So a player could try to go for all the different outcomes, and thus Aoi's character would have all the different guys.

Aoi nodded along. "So you think it would be a good match for me?"

"Yes! It would be awesome if there was an ending like in the manga series, where you're with all five guys. I think people would be disappointed if that wasn't an option too."

"I think there is."

There were so many scripts, they'd started to blur together, but Aoi vaguely remembered doodling five dicks on a page with his character's face wide-eyed with them all.

Michiko flipped to the end of the script and read. A cute yelp left her, and Aoi had to hide his laughter.

"This will be perfect," Michiko said.

"I'll go with that one, then."

The door opened, and Sato came in, holding his briefcase in one hand. He did a double take once he caught site of Michiko, but then the shocked expression quickly melted into a warm glow. Both siblings could heat up a cold winter's day with their smiles.

Sato pushed up his glasses. "Did Aoi finally ask for your help?"

"Of course he did. It's not like you could help him with anything but robots. You should've asked for my help before you guys were drowning in scripts." Michiko gave her brother a hug. "It's sad that your boyfriend is the one that calls me and not my own brother."

"Work has me busy."

"Sometimes I think you just don't want to talk to me."

Sato looked at Aoi as Michiko squeezed him tighter. "What script did you decide on?"

"The one where Aoi gets screwed by everyone."

Sato cocked an eyebrow. "Really?"

A wave of heat flushed through Aoi's body. He cleared his throat, not understanding how Michiko and Sato could have grown up in the same household. Sato was so reserved, and Michiko could run a boys'-love convention by herself with how much energy she possessed.

"We went with the game script," Aoi said.

"It should be fun to do something different like that," Sato said.

Michiko finally let go of Sato and pulled on her coat. "I should get going so Aoi can welcome you home properly, but there's something our parents wanted to give you two. I figured I'd hand deliver it for them."

She dug through her purse then pulled out a red envelope. "Happy New Year" was written in heavy gold calligraphy across it, and there was a thick decorative cording wrapped around the invitation just to add to the formality.

"They want you and Aoi to come over for New Year's," Michiko said.

Aoi's eyes narrowed, and he took a step back. "What?"

"They want you both to come. You'll go with us to the shrine and everything, Aoi."

"That can't be true. Your mother hates me."

It was the first time Aoi had seen Michiko give a smile that didn't meet her eyes. "I know Mom was a little shaken when Sato came out, but I've been talking to her about it at least once a week, and I think once she really sees how happy you've made him, she'll come around."

Aoi bit his lip. "I d-don't think I can."

Sato frowned, and it crushed Aoi's heart. Sato didn't understand how impossible even the thought of facing his parents again was. All of Aoi's muscles told him to snatch the invitation and throw it out the window so they could pretend the whole thing never happened. It would be better than any future the alternative held.

"We'll talk about this later," Sato said. "Thanks for helping him out, Michiko."

THE YEAR OF THE MONKEY

(BONUS STORY)

AOI'S GUT TWISTED LIKE the pages of his scripts after a long day of recording. He couldn't escape New Year's, but maybe it wouldn't find him underneath the warm kotatsu table.

He lay on the wooden floor trying to ease his flopping stomach, but even the red glow from the table's built-in heater reminded him of New Year's fireworks. He groaned and traced the grained loops of the floor.

Everything had turned into such a mess because of him. It would be easier if Sato went to his parents' by himself.

The front door opened.

"I'm home," Sato called.

"Welcome home," Aoi greeted his boyfriend.

"Where are you?"

Aoi wiggled a hand out from under the blanket that trapped the heat underneath the table. "I'm under here."

The cold air stung, and Aoi drew his hand back into the warm cavern the kotatsu created. Aoi had no idea how he'd survived winter all these years without one.

The wooden floor vibrated under Sato's slippered footsteps. They stopped as Sato grabbed the edge of the blanket and lifted it. Aoi smiled at him even though he was letting all the warm air out.

Sato pushed up his glasses. "I wish I could fit under there."

"My top half was getting cold."

"You could've turned on the space heater."

"I didn't want to run up the electric bill."

"We can afford for you to be warm."

Aoi squirmed out from under the table and tugged on the lapel of Sato's blue suit. "But you can warm me up faster than any heater."

A flush stained Sato's cheeks. Even after two years together, he'd still sometimes blush at small innuendos. At least they didn't go over his head anymore like when they'd first dated.

The fine lines around Sato's eyes deepened. Aoi loved watching the lines grow with each smile he could coax out of Sato. Perhaps his tedious number crunching at his accounting job helped with some of the wrinkles, but when Aoi looked he could only see himself reflected in Sato's glasses.

That's all Aoi needed during New Year's—only Sato. No parents necessary.

"Are you still cold?" Sato asked.

"Very."

"You know, I can help with that."

Aoi hooked his finger on Sato's blazer and plucked the button free. Even though it had been just a few hours since Sato had left for work, their time apart had stretched into forever for Aoi. His hands slipped inside Sato's open jacket and wrapped around his hips. Aoi would make Sato wish his New Year's vacation lasted longer than a week.

"Why don't you show me, then?" Aoi licked his lips.

Sato bent down, and Aoi stood on his tiptoes to meet the kiss. Sato was too freakishly tall to kiss without a ladder. Sure, Aoi had stopped growing in upper primary school, but Sato could kneel for a kiss every once in awhile. Still, even with the awkward positioning, the gentle kiss made Aoi's muscles slacken and his stomach calm.

"Is that Jin's invitation?" Sato pointed to the paper on the table. "The colors kind of remind me of the Fire Tiger mecha suit. Does he like Gundam too?"

Aoi sighed.

Sometimes dating a nerd was hard. Aoi might've had a small infatuation with boys' love manga comic books, but at least half of that came from his job as a voice actor. Not to mention Aoi's books didn't take up as much room as the robot-filled glass display cases lining the walls.

"Jin hasn't seen any Gundam unless it was a porn parody," Aoi said. "Oh." Aoi ran his fingers through his blond hair and glared at the two invitations resting on the table. Jin's postcard was normal. An orange monkey smiled against a red-and-black background. "Jin's Awesome Orphans New Year's Party" was scrawled over the front.

It wasn't Jin's invitation that had driven Aoi under the table, but the other one with "Happy New Year" written in shiny gold calligraphy on a red envelope. Heavy decorative cording wrapped around the invitation just to add to the formality of what a visit to Sato's parents would be like.

Aoi had met Sato's parents when he'd tagged along for support as Sato came out to his parents. Sato had turned around and introduced Aoi as the man he loved. Sato's mother had run off crying, and though his dad had lingered a bit more to chat, the disappointment had been apparent on his face.

Aoi got it. It wasn't like his parents approved either.

"Did you stay underneath the table all day?" Sato loosened his tie.

Aoi couldn't say yes or else he'd look lazy while Sato worked all day. "I did some reading."

"That's better than the last-minute New Year's rush getting accounts settled."

"At least you're on holiday now."

Sato's fingers trailed down Aoi's spine. "It'll be nice to spend the time together and we can visit my parents."

Aoi rubbed his neck. "I don't know if I can see your parents."

"What?"

"Jin invited me to his party." Aoi had gone every year since he'd become friends with Jin. He threw a party for everyone in the music scene who couldn't go home, and Aoi had been number one on that list even if his only musical contribution was moaning in one of Jin's songs.

Sato picked up Jin's invitation and read over the back. "Jin's is New Year's Eve, and I always visit my parents New Year's Day."

"Oh." There went one way to get out of visiting Sato's parents.

"Weren't you just telling me yesterday that people go to Jin's parties to hook up?"

"It's not like *I'm* going to do that, but I've always made the New Year's soba."

Sato pushed up his glasses. "So make some soba, come home at a somewhat decent time, and then the next day, we go to my parents."

"They'd rather see you."

"When Michiko gave us the invitation, she said they wanted us both to come."

Aoi shook his head and grabbed the ingredients for dinner out of the fridge. After a quick rinse, he chopped up a radish.

"Come on," Aoi said. "You and I both know she misspoke. They don't want to see me."

"My parents knew I wouldn't go unless you were invited."

"But New Year's is such a family holiday. I'd be a third wheel."

Sato pressed his hand against Aoi's shoulders. "We're a family. I love you, and if they can't accept it, then I don't need them in my life."

Aoi muscles tensed. Sato didn't understand. His parents still contacted him. Aoi continued to hack away at the radish.

Sato wrapped his arms around Aoi, careful to avoid the chopping. "Why don't we actually open the invitation and see what it says?"

"Fine."

Sato grabbed the decorative envelope and pushed it to Aoi. "You open it."

"But they're your parents."

"You're the one apprehensive about going."

Aoi gnawed on his lip. He blamed Sato's bossy attitude on the emotionless numbers on spreadsheets he'd stared at all day. He just had to enter comments and they'd do whatever he wanted. But Aoi grabbed the envelope, managed to work the fancy cords through the knots, and slipped it open. The embossed monkey design was a lot fancier than Jin's, and with that came much more formal and stiff language.

"See, look." Sato pointed. "It says you and I are welcome to come."

Aoi sighed. "I guess so."

"Mom had to go the department store to get one this fancy. So she must be starting to come around."

Aoi chopped the head off another radish. "Until I fuck up."

"You won't."

"Last time didn't end well."

"But this proves they're working on it. I know the last time we went wasn't perfect, but this is them trying. They'll never come around unless we meet them halfway."

"I don't even know what to call them."

Sato shrugged. "I always say Mom and Dad."

"I'm not calling them Mom and Dad."

"Okay, my Dad's Ken, and my mom is Emi."

"I can't call them by their first names."

"But we're family. We've lived together for a while now."

Aoi grabbed another bundle of radishes from the fridge. "I'm at least going to say Mr. Ken and Mrs. Emi."

"Are we having radish soup for dinner?"

"What? No." Aoi looked down. He'd diced up at least a dozen radishes. "We are now."

ROCK MUSIC THUMPED ACROSS the apartment hallway. Somehow Jin managed to throw his parties at least once every few months but still hadn't gotten kicked out for a noise complaint. Maybe his neighbors were fans, or the long months he was touring were enough to make up for it when he got back.

Aoi knocked on the door, and Jin answered. He stood slightly taller than Aoi, but everyone else would lump them both in the under-five-foot club. They shared the same bottle of blond hair dye, but Jin kept his hair past shoulders in a typical glam visual kei style, while Aoi's was shorter.

"It sounds like the party already started?" Aoi asked.

"Nah, I'm getting the set list together."

"So everyone will hear me moan again."

Jin rolled his eyes. "You know you like it when people hear you moan. Besides, that's the only song you're on. If I don't play it, people will get mad since it's a musicians-only party."

Aoi stepped inside while Jin went back to messing with his music player. The mountain of CDs surrounding him looked more like Everest than all the other New Year's parties Aoi could remember. Jin's little pug dog, Princess Potato, jumped around to the beat of the music. At least she wasn't barking or gnawing on Aoi's shoes.

"Are more people coming than usual?" Aoi asked.

"About the same. I'm digging back into the discography for a good laugh. I used to write such bad lyrics."

"Used to?"

Jin crossed his arms. "Don't be mean to the host, or I'll limit how much beer you can drink."

There had to be at least six cases of beer on the balcony, and no doubt some of the guests would bring more. Really all Aoi had to do was talk about Jin's drummer, and he'd be too distracted lamenting the fact the he was straight.

"Did you forget I'm the one making all the food?" Aoi asked.

"Then start chopping. It wouldn't be New Year's without the soba noodles."

The kitchenette in Jin's studio apartment didn't allow for much cooking space, but Aoi had whipped up more elaborate meals than noodles when he and Jin were roommates.

Aoi got to work making the stock, while Jin messed around with his CDs. He sang along to half a song, then changed to a new one.

No amount of Jin's singing could distract Aoi. Through each cut of fish cake, his muscles tensed more. Usually cooking would slice away at his tension, but inside, he cringed like having to read bad dialogue from a script.

"So you staying the whole night or you gotta cut out early?" Jin asked.

"I have to see Sato's parents tomorrow. So not too late."

Jin whistled. "You're spending New Year's with them? That's a big step."

Aoi stomach curled; even chopping the scallions didn't help settle it.

"Has he been back to his parents' since the big coming out?" Jin asked.

"He refused to see them unless they welcomed me too. So if I decided not to go, I'd have double the guilt."

"I knew he'd be the best boyfriend you ever had."

Princess Potato danced around Aoi's feet. She was too peppy for the rock music playing and much too happy for Aoi's mood.

"Good thing you came early so you wouldn't be stuck in the kitchen and miss the party," Jin said.

"Then I'd miss out when you try to play matchmaker with everyone."

"I have a sixth sense about that kind of thing." "And you're single because...?"

"I need a man that can accept me and the princess in my life." Jin squatted down and petted the dog. She flopped on her back and snorted. "You're such a good dog. Yes, you are..."

"Can you get Her Highness out of here so I can cook?" Aoi sliced through another scallion. "Wait, that's a perfect idea."

"Exactly, you and Sato could get a dog that doesn't chew his figures. Then Princess Potato and it can go on walks together."

"What? No!"

"But it sounds sweet. We could post pictures online. The fans would love it."

"The only fans I care about right now are Sato's parents."

Jin leaned against the counter. "It's too bad you can't just hide out in the kitchen and cook for them."

"I can make mochi rice cakes. Everyone loves them, and Sato's parents can take out their anger out on the rice when they hit it."

Jin crossed his arms. "You mean we could've been eating mochi for years on top of soba?"

"You need to have an outdoor area to make it the traditional way."

"Wow, you really go all out."

"It tastes better that way."

"You can get into his parents' hearts through their stomachs."

Aoi laughed. "Then I can avoid all the awkward conversation."

"You got all the stuff for it?"

"Shit." Aoi dropped the knife on the cutting board. "I need a wooden bucket, the mallets, and the rice."

Jin pulled out his phone. "Don't worry, I'll make mochi-making supplies the required fee for the party."

Aoi crossed his arms. "Jin."

"Hey, my parties are the talk of the music scene. Everyone wants to come…" Jin stifled his own giggle, and Aoi rolled his eyes. "You know, even the fans catch wind of them. You should read the fan fiction."

"I basically read that stuff for a living."

"One of them there was an orgy between sixteen of us. Sixteen! What do we look like, a Korean pop group? It was hilarious."

"Shouldn't you be calling?"

Aoi finished chopping up the rest of the vegetables while Jin texted on his phone. He let out a few snickering giggles here and there, but by the time Aoi finished, Jin had slipped his phone in his pocket.

"You feel better about going now?" Jin asked.

Aoi shrugged. "Hand me a beer. I still want to forget what I have to do tomorrow."

Jin grabbed a beer out from the stack on the balcony. Princess Potato jumped and barked around before following Jin back in. Jin handed one to Aoi and kept one for himself.

"To impressing your boyfriend's parents." Jin held out his beer bottle.

"If I don't make his mother cry again, I'll count it as a success."

Aoi clicked his beer against Jin's and chugged it down. If he could survive tomorrow, it would be a miracle.

AOI HUGGED THE WOODEN mochi-making bucket. Two of the long wooden mallets stuck out of it while the mochi rice bags helped keep everything steady. Aoi balanced the bucket on his hip and fished the keys out of his pocket. He failed the first time, and the second time, and by the third he was ready to kick the door until Sato opened it. His sixth beer had been too much, but he stumbled into the apartment with his fourth attempt.

The door slammed shut behind him.

Shit.

He slipped out of his shoes, but his big toe caught against the edge of the vestibule step. He fell, and the bucket bounced off the floor, the heavy mallet slamming down next to it.

Fuck.

Pain pulsed through his toe to the back of his heel. He grabbed it, dulling the ache, but it didn't go away.

"Aoi?" Sato asked from the bed.

Aoi gnawed on his lip. He hadn't meant to wake Sato, but since he was...

"Your parents have a big enough yard to make a fire, yeah?"

Sato clicked on the bedside lamp, casting a huge shadow off his Gundam figures in their display cases. The plastic robots' shadows grew to the ceiling. Aoi would rather take his chances with them than with Sato's parents.

Sato slipped on his glasses. "What's all the noise?"

Aoi turned over the bucket and put the bags of rice inside. "Go back to sleep. I didn't mean to wake you."

"Am I dreaming or do you have a mallet?"

"I'm going to impress your parents by making mochi."

The bedsheets shuffled as Sato sat up. "You don't have to impress them."

Aoi swallowed, but his mouth remained dry. Sato didn't understand. Aoi had had sixteen years to impress his parents, but one dirty magazine and he was never welcomed into their lives again.

He dropped the bucket, but he didn't bother to pick it up.

"They already hate me for making their son gay."

Sato rubbed his forehead. "I was gay long before I met you."

Aoi dragged his feet all the way to the bed. He sat opposite Sato and rubbed his slick palms against the sheets.

"Your parents don't see it that way," Aoi said. "They see me as the guy who seduced their only son to the other side."

Sato chuckled and wrapped an arm around Aoi's waist. "Your moans are sexy, but I think there's a limit on what they can do."

The space heater in the bedroom clicked on, its red coils glowing.

"Your parents like mochi, right?"

"Go to sleep or you'll be too tired to make it for them."

"I used to make mochi with my parents. I just—I just want yours not to be like them." Aoi's voice cracked though his trembling lip.

He curled into a ball. His parents hadn't cared about his life, even after he'd made it as a successful voice actor. There was no point in hoping Sato's parents would be any different. Aoi had become the wedge between Sato and what had been a good relationship with his family.

Sato's warm body wrapped around him. Everything was so hot.

"It's going to be okay." Sato kissed the back of Aoi's neck.

"But what if they still hate me at the end of the day?"

Even being enveloped in Sato's arms didn't stop Aoi's thoughts from rushing. If Sato hadn't come out to his parents, then he could've continued to see them. Everything had been fine before.

Aoi pressed his face into his hands. "What if they decide to never speak to you again?"

"You make me so happy, and deep down that's all they care about."

"I thought my parents were that way too, but then they kicked me out."

Aoi rubbed the tears out of his eyes. He hoped Sato couldn't see, but Aoi's body trembled. Everything was ruined because of him.

"They invited both of us because you're a part of my life now, and they realize that." Aoi said nothing; any argument he wanted to make would be shot down by Sato. He could be too sweet for his own good.

AOI'S PHONE RANG, ITS glow cutting through the dimly lit apartment. Aoi groped for it, hoping to find it before it woke Sato.

A second ring.

Sato shifted and let out a sleepy groan. "What's that?"

Aoi snatched the phone, silencing the noise. He narrowed his eyes at the cherry blossom avatar popping up on the screen. What was Sato's sister doing calling him so early?

"Hello," Aoi whispered as he ducked into the bathroom.

"Come shopping with me," Michiko said, the usual pep in her voice.

"It's five in the morning."

Aoi rubbed his eyes. He'd hoped to get a run in before his funeral at Sato's parents. Aoi's head pounded, and even the bathroom light made his eyes ache. He shouldn't have had that last beer.

"If we don't start moving, all the good deals will be gone."

"I don't—"

"Come on, it'll be fun. I'll give you pointers about Mom and Dad."

Sato refused to tell him anything besides that his parents wanted him happy. If Aoi knew even a little more about them, it could turn everything around.

Aoi rubbed his face. "I'll go."

"You've already beaten Sato for the best brother of the year award, and we're not even related."

"It's only been the New Year for five hours."

"Shopping gives you double the points. So he'll have to work overtime to steal it from you."

Michiko rattled off where to meet, and as Aoi hung up, the bathroom door opened.

"Don't tell me you agreed to go shopping with her for those awful lucky pack grab bags," Sato said. "No one wanted the clothes to begin with. That's why you can't see what's in the bags before you buy."

His glasses were off, and his hair stuck out in pointed spikes like the robot heads of some of his figures.

"She's the only one in your family who likes me. Of course I'm going with her."

Sato yawned. "Go if you want, but you're missing out on New Year snuggles."

Aoi smiled and stood on his tiptoes to kiss Sato's neck. "Believe me. After this day is over, we're going to do a lot more than snuggle."

Sato's lopsided smiled melted Aoi's heart.

THE ADDRESS MICHIKO HAD given him led Aoi to the famous Shibuya 109 building. Of course she wanted to meet at what had to be the busiest shopping center in Tokyo.

Aoi held in a deep breath as the people crushed him to get to the deals. Everyone stood so much taller, so they bumped into him like he wasn't there. He slowly let out the breath, but the crowds never thinned and his nerves never untangled. New Year snuggles were looking better by the claustrophobic second.

He pulled out his phone. If he couldn't find her soon, he'd ditch the whole plan.

"Aoi!" Michiko called out.

Her bright pink floral jacket stuck out like a spring breeze in the dead of winter. A matching flower was secured to the side of her braided hair pinned to the top of her head like a crown. She pushed past everyone toward Aoi without a glance, but with her height people actually noticed she was there.

"I'm so glad you came," she said.

"You started without me." Aoi pointed to the two bags under Michiko's arm.

Michiko didn't answer; instead she turned her head and waved. "Mom's over there."

Aoi's mouth drooped. "You didn't say your mom was coming."

"You wouldn't have come if I had."

"You're damn right—"

The smile on Mrs. Emi's face grew into a frown the closer she got. Sato had inherited her eyes, but hers lacked the warm glow Aoi loved so much. He definitely should've stayed home.

She turned and smiled at Michiko. "There you are, dear. It's a good thing we're so tall, or else it would be impossible to spot you."

"Mom, you remember Aoi?" Michiko said.

She didn't even acknowledge Aoi. Instead she just cleared her throat and said, "What's the next store on the list?"

"Liz Lisa."

Aoi followed them even though Michiko was the only one who even looked at him. It would look a million times worse if he ditched now that Mrs. Emi had seen him.

They waited in line at the frilly clothing store with so many floral prints it could've doubled as a florist. Unlike the other stores whose luck packs were cloth bags, the eternally-stuck-in- spring store used luggage to conceal what the buyers were purchasing. People left with either a small floral carry-on or a large pink one that most airports would require to be checked in. Big or small, there were way too many zeros at the end of the price.

Michiko wheeled both types out of the store.

"Aoi, do you mind helping me with these?" Michiko asked. "They have wheels, so it's easy, but I already have three bags, and it's hard enough to get to the lucky packs with those."

"Sure, I don't mind."

After a few hours' shopping, he realized what Michiko really wanted him there for: to help carry everything. If it won any points with Sato's parents, he'd do it. During the next hour, Michiko or Mrs. Emi bought five more lucky packs from the different stores. Michiko would casually hand the bags over to Aoi. At first, they had been easy to stick on the luggage handle, but after a few bags they would tip over if Aoi didn't keep a tight grip on it. Eventually, Aoi had been bogged down with so many lucky packs, each step felt like a weight workout routine.

Every time Aoi caught a glance of Mrs. Emi, she frowned. If he couldn't win her over by carrying all their stuff, there was no way making mochi would do it.

Aoi bit his lip.

"Let's get one for your brother," Mrs. Emi said.

Together they strolled to a men's store, while Aoi took more lumbering steps. For once, the amount of staff outnumbered customers. The pressed collared dress shirts and ties reminded Aoi of Sato, expect for the few neon-colored ones with matching crazy-patterned shirts.

A large table contained the lucky packs. A group of them had an *M* tag sticking out of the cloth bags, and others were marked *L*.

Sato's mother grabbed a bag from the *L* stack.

"He's actually more of an M now," Aoi said. "It helps when he's not eating vending machine food."

Her lip curled. "But he's so tall."

Aoi swallowed. He didn't want to start anything, but it would be a waste of money if she bought the wrong size. He readjusted the bags on his shoulder, then played with one of the tags.

"There's always extra in the pants' hem for height adjustments," Aoi mumbled.

Michiko stepped closer to him. "What were you saying?"

"I've adjusted Sato's hems before," Aoi said. "It's a quick sew job. So fixing an *M* is easier than the *L*."

"You know how to hem things? That's so awesome!" She sounded like Aoi had bought the world's supply of floral fabric and given it all to her.

Aoi rubbed his neck. "It's not that hard."

"But no one knows it anymore, and you're an awesome cook on top of it. Are you cooking anything for New Year's?"

"I was thinking we could all make mochi."

"Homemade mochi!" She turned to her mom. "Doesn't that sound awesome?"

Mrs. Aki shrugged. "Perhaps."

There was no pleasing her. She grabbed the *M* bag and headed for the line. Aoi sighed and adjusted the straps of the bags on his shoulder.

A black tie with subtle green stripes stood on one of the display tables. It was the same color as Sato's favorite Gundam, or at least the one he'd chosen to be his favorite for the past few weeks.

Aoi picked up the box holding the tie and flipped it over. He cringed at the price, but the 20 percent off sign helped the blow. Even if it wasn't on sale, Sato was worth it. He could get his boyfriend a New Year's gift even if Sato had dragged him to his parents.

No one else had gotten in line, so Aoi stood behind Mrs. Emi.

Her shoulders tensed.

"Sato would've been better off if he'd never met you," she said under her breath, but loud enough for Aoi to hear.

AOI TRAILED A FEW feet behind Michiko and her mother as they walked the final block to their home. They chatted amongst themselves, but Aoi let the words drift away like the light snow falling around them. Mrs. Emi didn't want him there, and all Aoi's doubts had been right. He readjusted the lucky packs digging into his shoulders.

They entered the house, and Sato came out of the kitchen to greet them. For the first time in hours, Aoi smiled.

"You enjoyed the shopping?" Sato asked.

"It was a bit more of a workout than I expected." Aoi laughed.

Michiko slid off her shoes. "It's good to trade off between cardio and weight training."

Sato pushed up his glasses. "Spoken like a true gym manager. Are you trying to sell my boyfriend a gym membership?"

Michiko laughed, but her mother crossed her arms over her chest and grimaced. Sato frowned and Aoi looked to the floor. No matter how much Sato insisted Aoi spend with New Year's with his family. Aoi was still the tagalong boyfriend he'd been dating for only three years. Aoi didn't belong with them.

"Could you put the bags on the floor in the living room for me?" Michiko asked.

Sato grabbed half of the bags and helped Aoi carry them to the center of the room. The room hadn't changed since the '70s, but the family photos dotted on the furniture and hanging on the walls spanned the ages. Aoi rolled his shoulders, finally getting the feeling back in his fingers.

"Here, sit next to me." Sato patted the sofa beside him.

Aoi sat, but since Sato was in the corner, it meant one other member of the family would be stuck beside him. Michiko wasn't helping since she was putting the various bags into stacks.

"We got one for you too, Sato," Michiko said.

Sato chuckled. "Hopefully no lucky poop ties this year."

"Why don't you try on what you got for a change? It can be a sibling fashion runway."

He looked at Aoi, but before Sato could open his mouth, Michiko grabbed his arm and pulled him to the back rooms.

Aoi shuffled his feet, trying to find a good position for them, while Mrs. Emi stood on the other side of the room. The clock ticked on in their silence.

Sato's dad came out from the kitchen and gave Aoi a half smile. Aoi looked away and rubbed his palms on his pants. Having both parents in the room only made his anxiety worse.

"I'm going to go help Michiko," Mrs. Emi, then left.

At least Mr. Ken hadn't run into the other room, and his smile held a bit of promise behind it.

"You drink coffee?" he asked.

"Yes."

"Sugar, cinnamon?"

"Black is fine."

He disappeared into the kitchen for a minute, then handed Aoi a misshaped glass made of out of clay coils. The off-blue-colored mug had a few chips around the rim. It looked old but well loved. Aoi warmed his hand around the cup. His pinkie rubbed against the carved button, which read "Sato." He must've made it as some elementary art project.

Aoi cupped the mug a little tighter and wished Sato was there.

"My grandmother was from Taiwan," Sato's father said, "but once she came here, she loved homemade mochi. I can vaguely remember making it with her a few times when I was little."

"I made it every year back home."

"Sato told me you're a good cook."

Aoi pressed his lips together and took a sip of the coffee. "I tried to teach Sato a thing or two, but when he's not under supervision, we have to worry about the apartment burning down."

He laughed. "He gets that from me. I can only make coffee."

"This is good." Aoi took another sip of the coffee. "You'll have to show me how you made it."

"It's about getting whole beans and grinding them up at home."

"I see."

At least food could impress Sato's dad.

"The way Sato talks about you... I'm happy he found someone that makes him happy."

Warmth radiated throughout Aoi's body. It was like Mr. Ken had put all the affection he had for his son into the coffee and shared that love with Aoi. He accepted the two of them as a couple.

"Are you ready?" Michiko called from the other room.

"We are!" Mr. Ken said. "She's done this since we got her first lucky pack at thirteen."

Michiko came out first in a pink ruffle shirt and a short brown skirt. The items matched well considering they had been thrown together from the lucky pack. Mrs. Emi came around the corner and smiled and clapped while Michiko spun around and struck various poses. Mr. Ken joined in the celebration, and even Aoi lightly clapped against the coffee cup.

"Sato, it's your turn!" Michiko said when she left the runway.

He came out in a mustard-yellow shirt, blue plaid pants, and a pale pink tie. Not only did they not match, but they were about as opposite of Sato's usually blue suits and earth-toned shirts as possible.

"That's unfortunate," Mr. Ken said.

A slow giggle crept up Aoi's throat until he burst out in laughter. Sato's dad was the first to join, and then everyone, including Sato, was laughing.

"I don't think those clothes are you at all," Aoi said between fits.

Sato cracked a smile. "The pants might work for you, but they'd be way too long."

"The plaid is nice."

"I'm going to try on the next look." Michiko ran off to the back.

"I'll change out of this too."

Aoi was yet again alone with both of Sato's parents. While his dad sipped coffee, Sato's mother glared at him. Her words while they'd been shopping bounced in his head like a mic with bad reverb.

Sato would've had a better relationship with them if he'd never come out. Aoi knew if his own parents had never found out, then he wouldn't have had to fend for himself since he was sixteen. The thick tension in the air made it hard to breathe.

Aoi stood and found the nearest bathroom. He could hide out in there until Sato finished changing. Being beside him made dealing with his mother a little easier.

Aoi splashed water on his face and leaned against the counter. They weren't even halfway through the day and Aoi had to hide. There was no way he could make it through visiting the shrine for New Year's prayers and come back to make mochi after. He'd already told them he was making mochi, so it would make him look ten thousand times worse if he left without doing it.

"Are you okay?" Sato knocked on the door.

"I'm fine."

"You don't sound fine."

Aoi sighed.

"Can I come in?"

There was no escaping. Aoi couldn't hide in the bathroom to avoid Mrs. Emi's disgusted gaze the whole time Michiko put on her fashion show. At least he could spend a little time alone with Sato while they both hid in the bathroom.

Aoi opened the door. "I got you something, but I don't think it'll go with those plaid pants."

"What is it?"

Aoi stepped into the hallway and pulled out the wrapped package from his coat.

"I saw it in the store, and it made me think of you," Aoi said.

"They had something in the store that wasn't a lucky pack? Can you tell my sister that?"

Aoi laughed while Sato opened the package.

"I thought it looked like the Gundam you like? Death Wing..."

"It does have the same color scheme. This is awesome! I can actually wear this to work."

Sato wrapped his arms around Aoi and gave him a tight hug. All of Aoi's muscles grew tense. Sato had been pushing the unspoken no public displays of affection rule recently, but hugging at his parents' house was worse than all the other times put together.

Then what Aoi feared most happened.

His gaze locked with Sato's mother. Her mouth dropped open, and her eyes spoke of horror.

Aoi pulled away. "I need to go."

He snatched his coat and headed for the door, but Sato grabbed his hand and laced their fingers together.

Mrs. Emi gasped. "What are you doing? You can't do that in my house."

Aoi tugged his hand, but Sato wouldn't let go. They'd made a mistake, and it would be better if Aoi left. He needed to go. Sato should've known better. Why wasn't he letting him go?

"No. Mom you need to get used to Aoi being here and not shoot him dirty looks. Don't think I haven't noticed them," Sato said.

Michiko and Mr. Ken stood behind Mrs. Emi. Everyone was staring, but Sato still didn't let go. Instead he bent down and kissed Aoi's face. Not only did Aoi's cheeks grow hot, but his whole body radiated with embarrassment. Sato might've been comfortable enough to kiss in front of people, but Aoi wasn't anywhere near as close.

"If Michiko brought a boyfriend to tag along, you wouldn't care," Sato said.

Mrs. Emi crossed her arms. "That's different."

Mr. Ken shook his head and put a hand on his wife shoulder. "No, it's not. We talked about this, Emi."

"Did you see what they did? We can't allow it."

"Do you never want to see Sato again, because that's what's going to happen if you keep acting like this?"

Her lips thinned into a line, and Aoi's heart raced. Sato still hadn't let go, but listening to Mr. Ken's words, Aoi didn't mind Sato's grip as much.

"It's stupid to lose our son over something insignificant like this."

"Fine," she said between clenched teeth.

Sato squeezed Aoi's hand, but it didn't stop the pain welling up in the back of his throat. He didn't want to make Sato's parents angry.

"Let's get going to the shrine before it gets too crowded," Mr. Ken said.

Mrs. Emi uncrossed her arms. "Good. We all need to pray."

"GO GET THE BUCKET," Aoi said.

Sato hurried and brought the wooden bucket to Aoi. Steam drifted from the steel pot filled with the mochi rice. Its subtle sweetness lingered in the crisp air. Together they dumped the rice as Mr. Ken hovered around them.

Michiko came by to check in every so often, but she and her mom mostly stayed in the kitchen making different flavorings for the mochi. Aoi could glance in the kitchen window at the ladies talking. The occasional frown on Mrs. Emi's face made it clear what the conversations were about. At least Michiko was trying to convince her mother that Aoi hadn't destroyed Sato's life.

They couldn't make Sato's favorite of sweet red bean mochi since the beans would have needed to soak overnight, but they managed with soy sauce and fermented beans.

"What do we do next?" Sato asked.

"Grab the extra mallet and help me squish the rice together."

Aoi grabbed his, and together they squished the rice.

"I want to try." Mr. Ken took his son's mallet and helped Aoi.

Aoi smiled. Mr. Ken was better at it than Sato, and after a few minutes the rice came together in a doughlike sticky ball. The mallet grew heavy in his arms, but to be fair, the handle was almost as long as he was tall. He pulled back and wiped the light sweat off his forehead. Maybe he did need to add weight training to his work out.

Snow drifted over them, dusting their clothes, but with all the movement, Aoi stripped off his coat. He tossed it on top of a snow-covered bush along the back fence. The empty flower bed had probably flourished in the spring.

"Aren't you worried about catching a cold?" Mr. Ken asked, his eyebrows knitted together just like Sato's.

"I'll be fine. Now we have to hit it in the center and turn it until it's nice and marshmallow- like. Who wants to go first?" Aoi asked.

Sato pushed up his glasses. "Maybe you should show us."

Aoi's arms were already sore from the mallet, but being exposed to the cold temperature had numbed the ache a little.

"Okay, but don't laugh," Aki said.

"Why would we do that?"

Aoi didn't answer; instead he pulled the mallet back as far as he could and hammered into the rice. His height and admitted lack of upper body strength made only a tiny tap to the top of the rubbery balled rice.

Sato snickered. "Maybe it would be better if I try next."

"Good. If I'm stuck doing it, then we won't have mochi until next year."

Aoi stood back as Sato hit the mochi directly in the center. He leaned in and gave the rice a half turn, then waited for Sato to hit it again. They repeated the process for a few minutes. Then Sato's dad had a go, with his son turning the rice.

They worked well as a team and would trade off when one of them got tired. Michiko and her mother strolled out and watched. A smile spread across both their faces.

"You're doing good!" Mrs. Emi cheered.

Mr. Ken struck the rice again. "Aoi's a good teacher."

Aoi laughed. "Maybe not when it comes to actually hitting it."

They came and Mr. Ken explained to them what they were doing. Aoi smiled, because while making mochi, no one cared about his relationship with Sato. Everyone was too fixated on the mochi to even remember the tension between them.

"Michiko, you want to give it a go?" Aoi asked.

"I want to see Mom do it first."

"I don't—"

"Here, Mom." Sato handed the mallet over.

Her lips pursed, and Aoi bit the inside of his cheek.

"It's fun once you get started." Aoi said.

"Come on, Mom. We don't want to be party poopers," Michiko said, the tone in her voice making it clear what they'd talked about while making the flavorings.

"It's a good stress reliever," Mr. Ken said.

A half smile cracked through her sour face, and she took the mallet.

"Aim for the center," Aoi said.

Mrs. Emi's strike landed right in the center.

"Wow, very good!" Aoi cheered and turned the mochi over. "Okay, do it again."

Sato's mother ended up being the best mochi smasher of the family. Out of everyone, she had the most frustration to get out.

It took about ten more minutes of beating the mochi before Aoi proclaimed it done.

They brought the plate of mochi inside and split it up. Each person got their own plate of the chewy concoction and mixed in the various flavors.

"This is the best mochi I've had." Mr. Ken stuffed another glob in his mouth.

"Be careful to take small bites," Mrs. Emi said.

"I'm not that old yet. This is so much better than the stuff at the store. It's still warm and everything."

"Can we leave the mochi stuff here for next year?" Sato asked.

"Sounds delicious. You won't have to lug it on the train with you again," his dad said.

"So we can do it again?"

"I think it makes a good new tradition."

"Let's take a picture, then," Michiko said. "Oh, I left my phone in my coat."

"I'll go get it." Aoi stood.

He walked through the living room back to the coatrack. The mochi was a success with Sato's dad, but his mom still hadn't cared to have him there. Aoi shook his head and grabbed Michiko's phone, which was trapped in a rose-printed case. He should've known it would take more than cooking skills to win them over.

He took in a deep breath and put on his best smile when he came back to the dining room.

"Okay, everyone, scoot in close so I can take the pictures," Aoi said.

He snapped a few and swallowed the lump in his throat. Sato had a good family. Even if they hadn't welcomed Sato's orientation with open arms, they were trying, which was more than Aoi's parents had done.

"Aoi, why don't you get in the picture too," Mrs. Emi said.

Aoi's mouth dropped. "B—but I'm not really—"

"You're the reason why we have the mochi. It would be wrong not to have you in the photo."

"Come on, Aoi, set it on the counter with the time delay. That's how we usually do it."

Aoi rubbed his eyes and nodded, not trusting his voice enough to speak. He set up the phone and stood beside Sato. He threw an arm around Aoi's shoulder and squeezed as the phone blinked and took the photo. Aoi's cheeks hurt, he smiled so much.

They continued their meal and chatted. Mr. Ken told an embarrassing story about Sato's first visit to the eye doctor. He had kicked off his shoes and refused to get eye drops because a kid at school had said they'd blow up his eyes. Sato had wanted to keep his eyes just the way they were— even if they couldn't see the chalkboard, they were better than being in bits from exploding eye drops.

The sticky mochi made for quickly filled tummies. Mrs. Emi sectioned off the rest and put them in wrapped dishes.

She gave Aoi one. "The mochi was very good, and I look forward to when we do this again next year."

Even though it was formal and stiff, at least she sounded sincere.

Aoi bowed. "Thank you for allowing me to come."

"Well, I'd like to see my son, but you made a good addition to New Year. You'll have to go shopping with us next year too."

If carrying shopping bags and making mochi were the way into Mrs. Emi's heart, Aoi would do it every day.

Sato said his goodbyes, and they left the house smiling.

"See, that wasn't too bad, was it?" Sato said.

"Your mother actually looked happy at the end."

"It's because you're amazing."

Aoi glanced around to make sure they were alone, then planted a kiss on Sato's lips.

Aoi grinned. "Let's get home and ring in the New Year right."

JANUARY

SATO NEVER UNDERSTOOD HOW Aoi could create such delicious food without even needing a recipe. All the spreadsheets Sato drew up when he cooked had never worked.

For their New Year's dinner, Aoi had cooked everything from fermented daikon radishes to sweet black soybeans. Each dish had been more lavishly displayed in the lacquered bento box than the next. And somehow everything had tasted better than the next.

Sato stretched his legs underneath the kotatsu table and brushed his big toe along Aoi's socked foot. Aoi giggled and returned the touch.

"Everything was so good." Sato patted his stomach. "Maybe next year you can make the New Year's meal at my parents' place along with the mochi."

Aoi shook his head. "There's no way I'm going to make it for five people. It took me hours to cook these, and there's only two of us."

"But everyone will help out, so it won't take as long."

"It wouldn't have taken so long if you hadn't helped cut the carrots."

Sato held up his finger with a *Gundam*-themed Band-Aid wrapped around the tip. "So knives aren't my friend, but when I was younger, Mom would make the first meal of the year from scratch too. It was only when Michiko entered high school that she switched to getting store-bought bento. They're not as good as yours."

"I hope not."

"Dad would love your candied sardines."

Aoi rolled his eyes. "I care more about what you think than your parents."

"Well, they would think everything was wonderful like I did."

Aoi looked away, and Sato sighed. Perhaps he'd been pushing Aoi too far. They'd spent New Year's Day with Sato's family, so perhaps bringing it up again was too much too soon. But everything had gone so well. Sato didn't want Aoi to put up another fight when the next New Year's invitation came. Things wouldn't get less awkward between him and Sato's parents unless they—

"Maybe next year I'll make one less dish. Then we can enjoy dessert faster." Aoi licked his lips.

"I'm so full it sounds like a good idea," Sato said.

Aoi leaned back and stretched out on the floor. His hand slipped under his shirt, and a small moan escaped his parted lips. Sato leaned forward, getting a better view.

Aoi continued his petting, and all the while, his shirt rode up to expose more of his tummy. The skin between Aoi's sharp hipbone and the rough fabric of his jeans made Sato's cock stir. Aoi would taste better than the yuzu sorbet chilling in the freezer.

Heat pumped through Sato. They'd been together two years—well, if he counted the first time they'd met and not the weeks in which Aoi had played the friendship-kisses-are-a-thing game. Sato smiled. He couldn't imagine his life without Aoi by his side.

Aoi lifted his head and caught Sato staring. A grin appeared on Aoi's face, and he lifted his shirt a little more. Sato's cheeks flushed.

"My sardines weren't small?" Aoi asked.

"Well, they're sardines, so they—"

"So you're saying *my* sardine was just your size." Aoi rubbed down the length of Sato's foot with his toe. There was a strange glint in Aoi's eyes. Maybe his allergies were acting up again?

"I guess so?" Sato cocked an eyebrow.

Aoi groaned. "Sometimes I think you're just as bad at understanding my innuendos as the first time I met you in the *Gundam* section."

"I still can't believe I actually managed to speak to you."

"You thought I was still in high school."

Sato laughed. "I'm glad you corrected me about that."

Aoi squatted behind Sato and snaked his hand down his shirt. Sato cupped Aoi's hand over his heart through the shirt.

"Let's celebrate the New Year right." Aoi nipped at Sato's neck.

Sato leaned back into Aoi and pulled him down for a kiss.

"Then I get to have your big sardine in me?" Sato tried to get through the whole thing without laughing, but he couldn't.

"Okay, maybe it wasn't the best innuendo," Aoi said.

"It's okay because it was yours."

"You're so cheesy." Aoi tugged Sato toward the bed. "Don't worry about the dishes. You can do them later."

"But your pots might get residue."

Aoi's pots not retaining their bought-from-the-store-yesterday glow had been the bane of meals for Sato. After the last bite of a meal, Aoi would insist Sato clean them right away.

"The way a couple spends their first night of New Year sets the stage for the rest of the year," Aoi said huskily. "I'd rather not spend it watching you do dishes."

Aoi pushed Sato down on the bed then straddled his hips. Sato moaned as Aoi rubbed his clothed cock against Sato's. His toes curled, and he thrust upward for more friction.

Aoi caressed Sato's cheek then kissed him. The second Aoi's lips touched his, electricity shot between them like the first time. Sato opened up like he always did, allowing Aoi to dominate and consume him.

Sato's arms wrapped around Aoi and pulled him back down. Sato couldn't get enough of Aoi's lips on his or the way the smaller man's tongue curled around his in the most delicious way. He could toy with Sato all night with just his tongue, and Sato would never tire of it.

Aoi pulled away, getting a small moan out of the back of Sato's throat. Aoi grinned, slipped off Sato's glasses, and placed them on the nightstand. Then he pressed their faces together.

Nose next to nose.

Cheek against cheek.

The subtle connection felt better each time.

Aoi was the only person who got to feel Sato unprotected by the frames. He could let everything go and fall deep into his desire with Aoi.

Sato's hands snaked down Aoi's body and squeezed his ass. "Fuck me."

Aoi grinned. "If we do it, that means we'll do it every day this year."

"That doesn't sound too bad, but what happens if you have to stay the night for an in-store event?"

Aoi popped open the first button of Sato's shirt then kissed his way down, unbuttoning a new button with each word. "We'll just have to have phone sex."

Sato's cheeks grew hot, and each of the kisses Aoi planted on him burned. Phone sex was something new for them—but then everything in the bedroom with Aoi had been something new for him at one time or another.

Aoi undid Sato's pants and pulled out his hard cock. Aoi had the most marvelous way he twirled his tongue around the head of his length. Sato had no idea how he did it, and even when he went down on Aoi, he was sure he'd never be able to duplicate it.

"Aoi!" Sato gasped when he got close.

Aoi quickly let Sato's cock pop out of his mouth and grinned down at him. Aoi leaned back on the bed and stripped off his shirt in a deliberately slow fashion. Sato reached down and gave his length a few pumps.

"You look so hot when you do that," Aoi said.

Sato laughed. "You do it better."

"But when you do it yourself, it's like a buttoned-up salaryman coming undone. Everyone thinks the guy who moans for a living will take off his pants."

"You look just as good with them on as off."

Aoi grabbed one of Sato's legs and kissed it. "Do you want me to keep them on today?"

Sato gulped. They had once been in such a hurry that Aoi had kept his pants on. The rough jeans had rubbed against his legs and balls. Sometimes the zipper's teeth had caught on the fine hairs and tugged. Each of Aoi's thrusts had sent that much more pressure that Sato's world had exploded.

Sato let out a deep moan.

"I take that as a yes." Aoi licked his lips.

All of Sato's words left him, and he only wanted Aoi. Now.

Aoi kept his jeans on and grabbed the lube from the nightstand. He slathered his fingers and gently slid one into Sato. The small burn with entry soon faded and was replaced with a desperate need for more.

Aoi kissed Sato's thigh, his hair lightly dancing over Sato's neglected length. Sato widened his legs, silently begging for more. Then Aoi arched his fingers and touched that spot within Sato. He let out a string of moans, and Aoi joined him in a hum.

"You sound so wonderful," Aoi said.

"Stop teasing me."

Aoi licked up Sato's legs to his thigh and the little hairs around the base of Sato's cock then stopped. Aoi slid in another finger, and Sato swallowed it up.

"I'm not teasing you," Aoi said, pushing his fingers a little deeper with each word. "Your moans are the only ones I care about."

Sato couldn't count the times he'd doubted himself when they had sex, but Aoi reassured him each time. He slipped in a third finger while licking up Sato's length. Sato gasped then fell deep into a moan.

"See, so delicious," Aoi breathed.

"Aoi…"

"Are you ready for me?"

"I'm always ready for you."

Aoi chuckled. "I think I remember rehearsing that line with you."

He lubed up his cock, and Sato turned to watch. Aoi's cock was amazing, and when he finally slid it in, he craned to see it. But the second Aoi's head was inside, he couldn't concentrate anymore and let the feelings wash over him.

"How does my cock feel inside you?" Aoi whispered.

"So hot."

Aoi gave a small thrust of his hips, making sure Sato was comfortable before the thrust became steady.

"Harder," Sato pleaded.

Aoi obliged, increasing the pace. His pants scratched Sato's legs, making him want to open himself up more with each of Aoi's thrusts. Aoi drove deeper inside Sato then stopped to roll his hips before sending another thrust deep against his prostate.

"I'm gonna—"

Sato came, spilling his seed all over his and Aoi's stomachs. Sato never lasted long with Aoi.

"You feel so good," Aoi said.

He continued in a frantic pace, and Sato could only gaze at the glow surrounding Aoi. He bucked his hips one final time and filled Sato up.

Aoi lay beside him with an exhausted sigh.

"I love you, Masatomo," Aoi whispered.

Sato smiled. There had only been a handful of times Aoi had called him by his first name. Aoi had once confessed he didn't want to use it often in case he slipped up in public, but it only made the few times he'd said it more special.

Sato wrapped his arms around Aoi. "I love you too."

FEBRUARY

SATO SMILED TO HIMSELF as he entered the last line of data into the spreadsheet. He usually finished double- and triple-checking the numbers at least an hour or two after work officially ended, but today he'd finished with time to spare. Maybe he'd sacrificed enough hours to the spreadsheet god and he'd finally taken mercy on him.

He leaned back in his chair, opened one of the boxes of Valentine's Day obligation chocolate, and popped the candy in his mouth. The few female accountants were stuck giving a box out to each of the men, but in March, the ladies' desks would be towering with the chocolate from the men.

The milk chocolate coated Sato's mouth, and he closed his eyes with a satisfied hum. He'd probably be sick of sweets by the end of the week since Aoi's fans also sent him snacks. Last year his agent had delivered three huge mailbags worth of sweet- and savory-filled goodies. There'd probably be enough delivered this year that Aoi could deliver a box of chocolate to all the men in Tokyo who hadn't received any.

Sato popped another chocolate in his mouth. If he came home early, Aoi would probably be so shocked he'd forget all about the fan gifts. Sato could think of a lot sweeter things they could do besides eat chocolate.

He could probably even leave early and be okay. The government had been talking about passing laws regulating the amount of overtime someone could work. Sato didn't want to be another headline about a salaryman who'd overworked himself to death. Though, if he had to die, the anime studio would be a good place. He could haunt the building and still see his favorite shows.

"You're done?" Jiro popped his head over the cubicle wall.

Sato dropped the box of chocolate and typed away on the keyboard. "There are a few things I need to finish."

It was better to lie to Jiro than suffer through him talking about whatever inane topic fascinated him today until the end of work.

"But those projects aren't due until next week. You're ahead for once. Congratulations!" Jiro said.

Sato pushed up his glasses. "Thanks."

Sure, Sato got his work done on time, but somehow Jiro knew exactly what to say to the spreadsheet god so that his project, which was supposed to take a week, was finished in a few days. If only Sato knew his secret, then they'd be able to analyze the latest *Gundam* episodes and debate where the series was going too.

Jiro pointed to one of the figures on Sato's desk. "You got the chibi version of the unit G-3c."

Sato held up the reddish robot toy. The small size made the enemy Gundam cute compared to the plain look of its larger-model counterpart. Aoi had gotten it for him at one of the toy capsule machines on the way home from recording one day.

Sato set the figure next to one of the hero Gundams. "The good guys have to have something to battle."

Jiro sighed. "If only it were so easy to figure out what girls wanted. Chie *still* can't decide if she wants to go out for Valentine's Day or stay in."

"What did you do last year?"

"We went out. It was so expensive. My wallet still has a hole in it."

Sato laughed. "Was it good, though?"

"Best food I ate all year, but all those zeros. I don't know if it was worth it."

"Most of the expensive places are probably booked up. If you stay in, does that mean she'll cook for you?"

"I don't think I can convince her to make food on Valentine's Day even if I told her I'd cook on White Day."

Sato popped another chocolate in his mouth. "I didn't know you could cook."

"I'm okay."

"Aoi usually does the cooking for us."

Jiro's eyes grew wide. "Aoi?"

Damn it.

Sato bit his lip and rubbed his fingers over the decorative red wrapping of the chocolate box. Maybe if he ignored Jiro, he wouldn't have to get into details.

"How long have you been dating her?" Jiro asked.

Sato's heart thumped in his ears. Aoi was a unisex name, so he could play Aoi off as a woman, but then Jiro would eventually talk about having another double date. He couldn't convince Michiko to help out with one again.

"If she does the cooking, then it must mean you've gone out for a while?" Jiro asked. "Are you two living together? Why didn't you tell me? I thought we were friends."

The pounding in Sato's ears grew louder with each word Jiro spoke. Sato had always been on guard when he talked with Jiro. How could he let something slip after so many years of hiding? But Jiro was his best friend, and keeping such a huge part of his life secret for so many years nagged at Sato like an unbalanced column on a spreadsheet.

Sato let out a deep breath. Maybe it was time to tell Jiro the truth. Coming out to his parents had been the hardest thing in Sato's life, but he hadn't thought about coming out at work. There were some protection laws in Tokyo but nothing federal to prevent him from being fired just because he was gay.

He didn't want to keep hiding anymore. His feelings for Aoi were as any straight couple's would be. Sure, their relationship went against the norm, but it wasn't like he was asking for anything other couples didn't have. Sato couldn't keep up the lies anymore.

He stood up and leaned close to Jiro. "Follow me. There's something I need to say."

Sato made his way to the bathroom, and Jiro followed behind him. Each step Sato took, his heart slowed. He was doing the right thing, and nothing would stop him. They entered the white-and-steel space, and Sato double-checked that no one else was with them.

Jiro crossed his arms. "Why did you have to drag me to the bathroom to tell me something?"

"Look, I should've maybe said this before." Sato ran his fingers through his hair. "Michiko was—"

"She wasn't abusive, was she? You don't think it could happen to men, but it can. Why didn't you tell me sooner? I would've helped you out."

Sato sighed. "Michiko is my sister."

Jiro's mouth dropped. "That's kind of… you were dating your sister?"

"What? No! I wasn't dating my sister."

"Then why did you say you were?"

Somehow in the short trek to the bathroom, Sato had imagined a very different conversation with Jiro.

The automatic bathroom spray puffed out a floral pomegranate scent throughout the room. At least after thinking Sato was dating his sister, saying he was dating a man probably wouldn't be as much of a shock.

"I lied to you about dating Michiko because I was dating Aoi, my boyfriend."

"Boy…friend?"

"I'm gay, Jiro."

Jiro took a step back. "Oh."

His tone didn't sound promising. Sato pressed his lips together as the flower scent staled in the air. If Jiro had such a big issue with it, then Sato would be out a best friend—but Sato didn't need friends who couldn't accept him.

"Is that going to be an issue?" Sato asked.

"I'm just happy you're not dating your sister. It's just…"

"What?"

"How long have you known?"

Sato cracked a smile. "How long have you known you were straight?"

Jiro laughed. "Okay, I get it. I wish you had told me sooner. Did you not trust me or something?"

"I wasn't ready."

"I understand." Jiro put his hand on Sato's shoulder and gave it a squeeze. "We gotta stick together, or else I'm going to have no one to talk to at work."

"I think you'd find someone."

"But no one in the office is as close to knowing as much *Gundam* stuff as you. I wouldn't be able to bring up old obscure episodes, and that's half the fun of coming into the office."

"Don't worry. I won't keep any big secrets from you anymore, but, ah, can we can keep this between us?"

Jiro pretended to lock his lips with a key. "It's safe with me."

MARCH

THE BAG OF GROCERIES banged against Sato's briefcase as he climbed the stairs to his apartment. Sato wiggled his fingers, hoping to get the circulation back to his extremities. Perhaps he'd bought too many things, but he didn't know what spices they already had. If he'd poked around the kitchen, Aoi would've asked what he was doing, and it would've spoiled Aoi's birthday surprise.

Since they'd started living together, Aoi had cooked all their meals. Anytime Sato brought up ordering out, Aoi insisted he could make something better. It was true, but the guilt of watching his boyfriend cook day in and day out had eaten away at Sato.

When Sato offered to help, Aoi barely trusted him to put the rice in the cooker without supervision. Sato had watched Aoi cook enough times not to set the apartment on fire. Aoi even allowed Sato to cut vegetables sometimes.

Sato knocked on the door with his foot since his hands were tied up with bags.

Aoi answered and stared at Sato.

"You went shopping?" Aoi asked. "But we went a few days ago."

"It's for your birthday dinner," Sato said. "I have it all figured out so you don't have to do anything."

"Sato." Aoi crossed his arms.

"I made a spreadsheet with the times and everything."

"And you had one last year, and we still ordered pizza."

"This year is going to be different. You've been showing me around the kitchen."

"And you still hold the knife wrong."

"But I don't nick my fingers anymore."

Aoi grabbed one of the bags and peeked inside. "Why did you buy things we already had?"

"I didn't know."

"You could've called. Then you wouldn't have had to waste money getting double."

Sato pushed up his glasses, making sure one side rested a little higher than the other. Usually that stopped the twitchy eye Aoi got when he thought Sato wasn't being frugal enough.

"If I called and asked about ingredients, then it would've ruined the surprise," Sato said. "Aren't we supposed to replace spices every few months anyway?"

Aoi sighed, but the twitching stopped, so Sato counted it as a win. He brought his laptop into the kitchen and read over the recipe for the fiftieth time.

The fridge opened, and Sato tried not to notice Aoi's eyes boring a hole into his back.

"You bought eel and beef? They're not both for tonight, are they?" Aoi finally asked.

"The site said they go well together."

"We don't need two meats. It gets expensive."

"But it's your birthday dinner. You don't turn twenty-five every day."

Aoi ran his fingers down Sato's arm, distracting him so he could glare at the computer screen. "Your notes are longer than the recipe."

"I didn't want to celebrate your birthday over pizza dinner again."

"Then you should let me help."

"You can't help make your own birthday dinner."

"Fine, you cook, but I'm supervising."

"You've been working so hard lately and deserve a break, especially on your birthday. Go read a manga, and I'll do all the cooking." Sato took Aoi's hand and gave it a tight squeeze.

"You've been crazy busy with taxes too. Most nights, you have to microwave your food because you're coming home so late."

Sato bit his lip. "I want this to be special for you."

"But it is special when we cook together."

Aoi tugged on Sato's tie until he bent down into a slow kiss that made time stand still. They both had been so busy with the day-to-day. Before they lived together, Sato and Aoi would block out whole weekends dedicated to spending time with each other. Even if they were in the same room, it wasn't the same.

Sato cupped Aoi's face and pulled away. "You mean everything to me."

"Then let's cook together like we did when we first moved in."

"Okay."

Aoi leaned forward and gave Sato a quick peck on the lips. "I'm sorry I've been so busy lately. There were just so many projects at once, and then all the in-store events usually happen during the weekends when you're off."

Sato pulled up his spreadsheet and took down the cutting board from the cabinet. "You don't have to say yes to everything."

Aoi gnawed on his lip. "But what if I have a dry spell one month?"

"We have enough in savings that even if we both lost our jobs, we could get by for a few months."

Aoi ran a peeled onion under cold water. "I like knowing I'm contributing to the bills."

"With how stuffed our mailbox is with scripts each week, I don't think you have to worry."

Aoi laughed. "So does that mean you can have two proteins for your birthday dinner?"

Sato pressed his lips together. "Mom asked me to have my birthday dinner over there."

"Oh, that's fine. We'll celebrate it when you get home."

Sato reached out and took Aoi's hand. "I want you there."

"But your parents don't."

"Mom knows I won't spend time with them unless you're welcome to join."

"She might say she does, but she doesn't really want me there."

Sato tugged Aoi into a hug. Sato knew he could never really understand what Aoi had gone through when he was kicked out of his home, but if Sato's parents were trying, Aoi could too. He'd never be more comfortable around them if he avoided it.

"She's trying. It'll take some time, and she wasn't that bad during New Year."

"She didn't mean a word she said. I could tell by the tone in her voice."

Aoi might've studied people's voices, but Sato knew his mother. She wouldn't say anything she didn't mean.

"What if we have it at a restaurant? Michiko can come and talk Mom's ear off," Sato asked.

Aoi bent his head, and his fair fell over his eyes. His hands tensed into fists, and then his whole body tensed, and it broke Sato's heart. Yet if they didn't try to resolve the issue, it would stay the same.

"What if I let you pick out the restaurant?" Sato said.

"Fine."

Sato brushed his hand against Aoi's until his fist came undone and their fingers interlaced.

"Let's start dinner, and I can give you my other birthday present," Sato said.

Aoi raised an eyebrow. "Oh? What is it?"

"You know what it is."

Aoi outlined Sato's lips with his fingers. The faint smell of onion lingering in the air. "But I like hearing you say it."

Sato's cheeks flushed.

"You sound so sexy when you talk dirty to me."

Sato laughed. If anyone was the master of talking dirty, it was Aoi, but the words of encouragement always pushed Sato a little further along.

"You'll get my big, hard cock," Sato whispered.

"Are you going to wrap it with a bow?"

"I'd do anything for you."

APRIL

AOI'S MUSCLES TENSED. IT was a horrible idea. He should've faked a cold and stayed home, but then Sato would've rejected all of Aoi's advances to give Sato the best birthday sex of his now twenty-eight years of life. Worst of all, Sato had been so determined to have Aoi tag along to celebrate his birthday with Sato's family, he probably would've rescheduled it for a different day.

Aoi trailed behind Sato as they entered the conveyor-belt-sushi restaurant. Aoi had picked it hoping the atmosphere of selecting sushi as it passed would distract everyone from their relationship. They wouldn't have to worry about waiting around for the check or anything because so much was automated in the restaurant chain.

"Happy birthday!" Michiko hugged her brother then did the same to Aoi.

Michiko's hugs were like falling into a field of flowers; her chiffon dress put any cherry tree to shame. Aoi had finally gotten used to them. Sato's mother, Mrs. Emi, and his dad, Mr. Ken, greeted them. Thankfully no awkward hugs were exchanged.

Sato answered the standard parental questions, and their number was called for them to dine. Sato slid in at the end of the booth with Michiko joining on the opposite side, placing her bright-pink gift bag with equally bright lime-green tissue paper on the table. Mr. Ken and Mrs. Emi sat on Michiko's side, leaving Aoi to sit directly in front of them.

Tea was offered, and from there, the waiter left them alone to grab the sushi as it passed them by on the conveyor belt.

"The cherry blossoms are nice this year," Mrs. Emi said to Aoi.

At least she wasn't talking about how he'd ruined Sato's life.

Aoi rubbed his neck. "They are pretty."

Sato patted Aoi's knee under the table and rested his hand on it. Aoi's muscles tensed again, and he brushed off Sato's hand. It was bad enough to do something like that in public, but in front of his parents!

"Grab the tuna for me," Mr. Ken said.

Sato reached for the plate on the belt and pulled at the plate underneath the plastic shield. The shield popped open, and Sato handed the small plate to his father.

Michiko grabbed a few more plates and pushed them into the center of the table. Aoi dug into each passing plate of squid. If he stuck to the chewy options, he could go the whole meal without talking.

"Aoi packed an amazing lunch last weekend, and we viewed the cherry blossoms," Sato said.

Did he really have to bring up what they did on the weekends too? There was no way his parents could pretend Sato and Aoi were friends with Sato's constant reminders that they were together.

"That must've been nice. I've been meaning to take your mother."

"You should hurry up, or the blossoms will be gone soon," Michiko said.

"Some of the trees had already turned to leaves when we went."

Aoi stared at the swirls on the empty plate before him as he slowly chewed his squid. Sato wasn't going to make dinner easy for Aoi or his parents. Couldn't he talk about more neutral topics like *Gundam* or politics?

"How's work?" Mr. Ken asked.

Sato watched the belt for a second then grabbed a plate of pineapple. "The same. We're supposed to get a few new hires soon. They'll take a few of the extra projects that pile up."

"And you?" Mr. Emi asked Aoi.

Aoi pressed his lips together. Why were they talking to him? They'd only come for Sato. It would be easier if he and Sato's parents didn't talk to each other.

"Work is busy," Aoi said.

Michiko smiled. "He's going to be in a few things I'm really excited about!"

"Oh?"

Sato laughed. "I think Michiko would be excited for any-thing Aoi acts in."

"It's going to be a phone game, and it looks super fun."

"You'll have to show me how to play," Mr. Ken said.

Aoi's cheeks grew hot. "I think it's more of a game for girls."

Michiko slid the empty plate into the slot underneath the conveyor belt where the rest of the used plates disap-peared. "I'm sure some men would play it too."

Michiko wasn't helping the situation at all.

"I don't think we've sung 'Happy Birthday' yet," Aoi said. "Do you guys do that? My parents would make the whole restaurant sing every year."

Aoi sung the first few bars, and then the others joined. When they finished, they clapped.

"Here's your gift!" Michiko said.

She handed Sato the radioactive-strawberry–colored gift bag.

Sato smiled. "You shouldn't have."

"What kind of sister would I be if I didn't give my little brother gifts on his birthday? Go ahead and open it." She winked at Aoi. "I figured starting small would work best."

An electric shock ran down Aoi's spine with her smile, but it was too late. Sato pushed back the tissue paper and pulled out a Wartenberg pinwheel. It had been used at the start of a massive bondage scene in the opening of *My Master's Wish*. Sato held it up and ran the pointy pinwheel part over his fingers.

"It's like for pizza?" he asked.

"Yes!" Aoi snatched it away and answered before Michiko could correct him.

"Thanks, sis. We can make it at home and not order out so much."

"You could probably make other things than just pizza with that. Aoi knows all about it."

Michiko's words dissolved into the background when Aoi looked inside the bag in case Michiko had decided to be more generous. His breath caught in his throat, and he rubbed his eyes, unable to believe what he saw.

No one would really buy *that*, especially for their brother, especially knowing their parents would be dining with them. Yet even after a second and third look, it hadn't changed.

Only Michiko could find hot-pink heart-shaped anal beads.

"Is something else in there?" Sato asked.

Aoi snatched the bag shut. "Thanks so much, Michiko. It'll be good to show Sato how to cook pizza."

Michiko laughed. "Hope you guys get a lot of *cooking* done."

Aoi took in a deep breath, but Mr. Ken gave him an off look. He was supposed to be the one on Aoi's side. Not the one who shot him dirty looks when his daughter should be the one in trouble. Heat radiated from each of Aoi's pores, and the whole room felt on fire.

"I need to go to the restroom." Aoi stood and grabbed Michiko's gift just in case Sato decided to open it up and show everyone.

Bolting out the front exit would've been Aoi's preferred solution, but he couldn't do that to Sato. Yet when it came to Sato's parents, Aoi always ended up hiding in the bathroom.

He slid down the men's-room wall. Things would never get any easier. He hugged his legs and buried his face in his knees.

The minutes passed, but he couldn't go back out there and face Sato's parents. The door opened, but Aoi didn't look up. Who cared if some stranger thought he was odd. Aoi couldn't go back out there. It would be impossible to face Sato's parents.

"You okay?" Sato asked.

Aoi shook his head and winced to hold back the tears.

Sato sat too, his burning hand rubbing Aoi's back. It only made everything worse. He cared so much that his comfort only weighed Aoi down with more guilt.

"They keep this place really clean."

Again Aoi said nothing.

After a few minutes, Sato spoke again. "Tell me what's going on."

"Your sister is nuts," Aoi mumbled.

"I know she's kind of out there, but she's not going to tell our parents that you voice-act boys'-love stuff. She's known I was gay since I was eleven but never even hinted it to my parents."

"I don't get how you two can be related. You were so oblivious to anything about sex when I met you."

"I wasn't oblivious—I just thought someone as cool as you wouldn't want anything to do with me."

Sato's smile calmed Aoi more than any breathing technique. Why couldn't it just be them?

"When you're ready, you can tell me. Until then, I don't mind sitting here with you," Sato said.

Aoi sighed.

The minutes passed, and Sato tugged on Aoi's sleeve until he surrendered his hand. He laced their fingers together and gave them a tight squeeze. He was too good for him.

"That wasn't a pizza cutter Michiko gave you," Aoi finally said.

"What was it, then?"

"It's a toy used during BDSM."

"Oh."

"And that's only half of it." Aoi pointed to the bag. "She put anal beads in there too. Who does that? No wonder she scared off your first boyfriend."

Sato squeezed Aoi's hand. "I'm sorry about her."

"It's hard enough dealing with your parents, and now I have to worry about her. I thought she was on our side, and then she pulls a stunt like that!"

"I know this is hard for you, and I'm so happy you came. The next time we see my parents, I'll ask her to sit out until you're comfortable."

"Next time." Aoi groaned and put his head back down on his knees. "I don't have a relationship with my parents, and it's fine."

Sato rubbed his thumb against Aoi's palm. "I don't think it is."

"I don't need to reconnect with the people who kicked me out when I was a kid."

"Not like that." Sato pushed up his glasses and looked away. "I mean it's not okay because now you assume my parents are going to be the same. I know they didn't have a perfect reaction when I came out, but it wasn't like they screamed or blamed you for it. Has either one of them really said anything to you?"

Aoi sniffed and pressed his head against Sato's hand. Sato's mother had said Sato would've been better off if he'd never met Aoi during New Year's. She'd said it before they all went back and made mochi, but even though she had smiled at Aoi by the end of the day, he couldn't shake the memory.

He couldn't tell Sato what she'd said. He thought too much of his mother, and it would devastate the relationship he shared with both his parents.

Aoi licked his lips. "No, she hasn't said anything."

"See? Not everyone will be like your parents. If you're ready, let's go back out there."

Aoi sniffed and squeezed Sato's hand as they stood. "Sure."

"Don't worry. I can help you forget all about dinner once we get home."

Sato leaned forward and kissed Aoi. He tugged on Sato's sleeve and deepened the kiss on his tiptoes.

When they finally parted, Sato's glasses were askew and a big smudge had been smeared along one side.

"We're going to throw away the gifts Michiko gave you," Aoi said. "The last thing I want to do while screwing my boyfriend is think about his sister."

"Agreed."

Sato put a hand on Aoi's shoulder. "You ready?"

"Yeah."

"I know it's hard for you, but I'm so happy that you're trying."

"Don't worry—you'll be paying me back tonight."

MAY

AOI LEANED BACK IN the chair, arching his back and stretching his legs. A dull ache hugged his lower spine, but it didn't lessen with the movement. Aoi couldn't decide if he should blame the stiff hotel bed or the uncomfortable convention chairs.

"Are you having a good time?" Sato asked.

He'd asked it every few hours since they'd arrived at the hotel, and each time, it made Aoi love him a little more.

Aoi smiled. "It's nice to finally go to a convention and not have to hide out for most of it."

"That's not what I mean."

"It's nice to spend time with you doing something you enjoy."

Aoi might've preferred to spend his weekend tangled in bed with Sato, but the crowded *Gundam* convention wasn't bad. Over the years together, Sato's *Gundam* enthusiasm had worn off on Aoi, so he was able to keep up with some of the panels they attended. Sato didn't even seem to mind that Aoi occasionally looked like a total idiot when he mixed up the names of robots and series the times they'd strolled through the vendor area.

Perhaps Aoi could convince Sato the midnight panels wouldn't be as interesting as what he had planned for him in the hotel bed.

Sato poked at his phone and pulled up the event's schedule. "So after this there's a comparison panel between old mechs and modern-day design details. Do you want to go to that one, or would you rather see the workshop about building your own figures? I mean, you don't have to go to everything I do if there's something you'd rather do."

Aoi grinned. When the convention had posted their panel schedule months ago, Sato had printed the roster and used a detailed highlight system, which he'd then transferred to spreadsheets to rank each time slot by desirability. Sato had planned out each minute of the two-day convention, but he'd always asked Aoi if there was anything he'd rather do.

"This is fine," Aoi said.

Sato pushed up his glasses. "Thanks again for coming. I know robots aren't your thing."

"That's okay. I know boys'-love manga wasn't your thing, but now our apartment is full of them."

Sato couldn't be any cuter if he tried, and surrounded by everyone else there with the same obsession as his, he lit up more than the time Aoi had asked him for help making an Excel file.

"Have you built your own mech before?" Aoi asked. "At the showcase, those were all figures people had made themselves and not the same model kit you usually do."

"They're more creative than I could be."

"You should give it a try. Your Gundam could be the lord of spreadsheets. It can have little cells with numbers in it."

Sato laughed. "What would yours look like, then?"

"Mine would have a few accessories that aren't standard." Aoi grinned.

"Might be a bit shorter too."

"There's no getting around that, but the packaging would be huge."

Sato nodded along. "Yes, the package is very important."

"Yours would have a nice package too."

"Hmm."

"It would be my favorite package out of all the others."

They chatted about packages until someone sat beside them, but by then, the room had filled with the dull rumble of convention-goers. The packed ballroom ignited with their excitement, and it even made Aoi give a little cheer when the first slide of their PowerPoint was projected on the screen.

The room quieted as they began their PowerPoint presentation. The panelist lectured over everything from minute detail in color scheme variation to height. Aoi had no idea how they figured out the height of something drawn, but somehow they had.

Aoi bit back a yawn. The last thing he wanted was to look bored at something that Sato loved.

"I'm gonna get a drink," Aoi whispered then left the room.

People lingered in the halls, and a large group was debating about who would win between a Nightingale Gundam and the Force Wing X5. Aoi knew enough to know that they were from two different shows, but with the crowd forming, everyone had to add their opinion.

Aoi squeezed past the group and spent some time checking his phone. Nothing new on social media, or at least nothing worth reading. Too many fans were excited that he and Atsushi were acting together in a dating-sim game. Aoi gnawed on his lip. Maybe he could get his agent to discuss not doing any promo with him, but he was so popular it would mean a lot of good exposure to his fan base too.

Aoi looked up from his phone and caught the gaze of a woman. He smiled at her and nodded, but then her eyes grew wide and her mouth dropped.

"Excuse me, but are you…"

Aoi put a finger to his lips. "It's a secret."

She sealed her mouth and nodded. She took a step closer. Her *Gundam* shirt was from Sato's favorite series, so she couldn't be too bad. It wasn't like she could get on her phone and call the rest of the BL fangirl horde to loom over him.

"Could you sign?" she whispered.

She held her phone case up: Aoi's character from *My Master's Wish* hugging the leg of his master while he sat on the chair with a riding crop in hand.

"Sure," Aoi said between clenched teeth.

If anything, maybe the new dating sim would finally kill the popularity of *My Master's Wish*. Aoi signed right over Atsushi's character's head. Maybe not the best placement, but the small revenge had Aoi grinning.

"So you're into *Gundam* too?" she asked.

Aoi shrugged. "I've gotten more into it over the years."

"It would be so cool if there was a BL *Gundam* series you could act in!"

Aoi snorted. Sato would enjoy that. He'd turn their apartment into the number-one fan shrine to the series.

"Wouldn't the robots get in the way of the boys kissing?" Aoi said.

"There's time for both kissing and robots."

"Well, if there's scripts out there for one, I'll look into it."

She nodded. "I haven't seen any manga like that yet, but hey, sometimes they make original stuff."

"And it's not like fans aren't already putting pilots together."

Or at least that was what Aoi always did when the *Gundam* shows got bogged down with battles. There was plenty of *Gundam* boys'-love drama in every series Sato had him watch, even though there were female counterparts to pair with the guys. Aoi tugged at the lanyard holding his badge. He'd been gone so long Sato probably thought Aoi had fallen in the water fountain.

"I need to get going," Aoi said. "Could you wait until after the convention to tell anyone? I'm here with some friends and-"

"I understand."

They exchanged another smile and parted ways. Aoi headed back toward the panel, but the crowd outside had grown enough to block the path.

"Come on, guys," Sato said. "Everyone knows that it's not only about the Gundam, but the pilot operating it. You can't say Nightingale is a better Gundam because, and I think we all can agree, Toshi isn't as good a pilot as Hana."

Aoi crossed his arms and leaned against the wall as Sato won over the crowd with the finer points of the characters' individual fighting styles. Everyone listened, then someone else spoke up, igniting a new debate about the best fighter regardless of suit.

Sato and Aoi's gazes met, and Sato managed to snake through the horde to where Aoi stood.

"You okay?" Sato asked.

"Yeah, I'm fine. Why do you ask?"

"Usually you go to the bathroom when something's wrong." Sato pushed up his glasses. "I wanted to make sure everything was all right."

Aoi wanted to reach out and embrace Sato to show him that nothing was wrong, but in public, such a display would be impossible. Even in the large crowd, someone would notice, and it would be devastating to his career if that woman managed to snap a picture of it.

"Let's get back to the panel before the people out here convince you to put on an unofficial panel about the pilots' different fighting styles," Aoi said.

Sato smiled. "That would be interesting, but unofficial panels are against the rules."

"Then you definitely don't want to give the horde any ideas."

They weaved through the crowd and back to their seats. All the while, Aoi imagined robots kissing.

JUNE

AOI'S FINGERS CURLED INTO a fist when Atsushi entered the waiting room.

The initial recording for the dating-simulation game *Nephilim Boys' School* finished weeks ago. It had been nothing but him and a mountain of lines with him alone in the recording. It had been perfect, but Aoi should've known it wouldn't last.

When the first press release announced the voice acting cast, the boys'-love fans exploded with joy. Not since *My Master's Wish* had Aoi and Atsushi been together, and everyone wanted them to be paired up again.

The producers would've been stupid if they hadn't written in a few more scenes with their characters together. But the tight recording schedule meant it would be easier if he and Atsushi recorded their lines together.

"What a pleasure to see you again." Atsushi brushed back his long hair.

His stupid voice was deeper than Aoi remembered. No wonder all the ladies loved him. If Aoi didn't want to punch him in the face each time they'd met, he'd be weak in the knees over Atsushi's voice too.

Aoi crossed his arms. "Of course I'm here. It's my job."

"Congratulations. Your moans put you at number one for playing bottoms last year. You think this performance will secure your spot this year too?"

Aoi rolled his eyes. "Those are just popularity contests anyway."

A popularity contest Aoi had hoped to rank in since he'd started voice acting. The only reason he'd even ended up in the top-ten charts was because of his work with Atsushi. The bastard's popularity rubbed off on him, no doubt.

Anytime he interacted with Atsushi, it left a bitter taste in Aoi's mouth, like he'd accidentally let a fish grill too long and the skin was more burned than edible. How could he not hate Atsushi after he'd locked them in a room together and almost made him miss his first Christmas Eve with Sato?

"You know, if you told everyone you're gay, you'd win all the popularity contests," Atsushi said.

Aoi rubbed his fingernail along the edge of the thin script. "I don't know what you're talking about."

"Good thing you play characters who aren't meant to believe the lies they tell themselves."

Aoi's jaw clenched. The sound check was taking forever, but Aoi wouldn't put it past Atsushi to have told the production team he needed an extra five minutes to torment Aoi.

Atsushi continued, "If you think working with me jump-started your career, see what happens after you come out. When I came out as bi, it did wonders for me."

Aoi stood and crushed the script in his fist. He'd hit Atsushi for locking him in that room, and it took everything Aoi had not to smack him in the jaw again.

"Where are you going?" Atsushi asked.

"The fuck away from you. The director can get me when he's ready."

"I'm only trying to help you out."

Aoi bit his tongue to stop his reply. Atsushi would just say something else to get the last word in. It was better to walk away and ignore the annoying prick.

Aoi found an empty hall nearby and leaned against a wall.

Atsushi almost sounded like Sato with the way he kept talking about coming out. When Aoi's parents had found he was gay, they dumped all his belongings outside the house and never let him return. It wasn't that Sato ever pushed Aoi to come out, but the whole year, Sato had been opening up to everyone. Aoi shook his head. It was too dangerous of a line for him to walk when it came to his job.

He pulled out his phone, but every social media site he poked around made his muscles tighten. Every comment and post he'd been tagged in were all covering the release of the game. Aoi groaned. He needed to create a personal account sometime, but he worried about snapping a cute photo of him and Sato and accidently posting it in the wrong account.

He clicked open his messenger. Sato would be at work, so texting him to complain about how much of an ass Atsushi was wouldn't be appropriate. Ten o'clock might be a bit early for Jin. When they'd roomed together, his rock-star life had seen anything before noon as too early. If anything, maybe he'd still be awake from the day before.

What do you do when you hate the person you have to work with? Aoi texted.

A few seconds later, his phone buzzed with Jin's reply. *Write lyrics obviously directed at them?*

Aoi grinned, surprised Jin was coherent enough to string together a sentence.

Can't, Aoi typed. *Gotta read what's on the script.*

They don't ad-lib like in movies sometimes?

Then the mouths wouldn't match up.

Oh, then kick him in the crotch on the way out, Jin typed.

Aoi snorted. *Very rock and roll.*

"Hey, Aoi! They're ready for us," Atsushi called.

Aoi looked up, and then Atsushi snapped a photo.

"Recording with Aoi," Atsushi said, typing on his phone. "Hashtag friends for life."

Aoi's phone lit up from the notification. He clicked on the newly uploaded photo of him on Atsushi's page. The post already had ten hearts and a few comments. How could he be so popular?

"That alone should get you at least twenty more followers by the time recording is over. You know how many companies want me to advertise for them, or the number of new voice actors who ask if I'll post a photo with them?"

Even if Aoi had already received three new followers, Atsushi was still a narcissistic jerk.

"Are they really ready for us, or are you just being an asshole?" Aoi asked.

"You should thank me for wanting to help you with your career so much."

"I didn't ask for your help."

"But you needed it."

Aoi ignored him and walked back to the waiting room. By then, the director was ready for them and rushed Aoi and Atsushi into different recording booths.

There were no hiccups the first hour of recording. The director wanted a few takes of all the lines and gave directions well. Atsushi disappeared and became the character that Aoi wanted. His cool voice drove Aoi's character to wet dreams.

The director's voice came over the headset. "Guys, I gotta take this call. So let's take five, okay?"

Aoi stretched his sore muscles from being stuck in one place so long as best he could in the small booth.

"Hey, Aoi." Atsushi's voice came through Aoi's headphones. "Do you think most people will try to get your character to go with mine?"

Aoi ignored him and continued his stretching. There was some leftover pork from last night; maybe he could make a quick stir-fry for dinner. Sato had been getting better at chopping vegetables. It was probably time to move him up to actually teaching him how to assemble a meal.

"I was listening to one of your past drama CDs, and you really do have a good moan," Atsushi continued to rattle on.

Aoi rolled his eyes.

"Do you jack off during the recording to sound so good?"

Aoi pulled off the headphones and left the recording booth as Atsushi continued talking. Aoi ran to the nearest bathroom and locked the door behind him. He turned on his phone and splashed some water on his face while it started.

Why did he always end up running into bathrooms? At least there was something comforting in the brushed-gray-and-white tiles. They were clean, and he could lock Atsushi out.

Aoi grabbed his phone and ignored the hundred or so little notifications that popped up beside the various social media apps.

He groaned.

If he never had to work with Atsushi again, it would be too soon. Aoi bit his lip, finger hovering over his text conversation with Jin. He wouldn't be able to help.

Aoi called Sato. He tapped his foot while the phone rang. He was working. It wasn't right to bother him at work, but Aoi's heart ached.

"Hey, is everything okay?"

The moment Sato's voice came over the line, it was like one of his warm hugs wrapped around Aoi.

"E-Everything's fine," Aoi said, but his voice shook.

"It sounds like you're having a bad day."

"Yeah…"

"Atsushi's being a jerkface again?" Sato asked.

A faint smile crossed Aoi's face at hearing Sato say "jerkface."

"He's the biggest jerkface I've ever met," Aoi said.

"When do you get off for lunch?"

"I don't know. Maybe an hour?"

"Then let's go to lunch."

Aoi rubbed his free hand on his jeans. "What if someone sees? There's so much hype around this game and—"

"Then we can go to a maid café. No pictures allowed there, and it would look like we're there for the maids."

Aoi laughed. "A maid café? Really?"

"Why not? It solves the problem of people seeing us together, and they're trained to make people laugh. It sounds like you could use someone to make you happy."

"I already have someone that makes me happy."

JULY

SATO LICKED HIS LIPS. "You look amazing in a yukata."

Aoi sighed. "I think it would've been easier if you'd bought mine from the kids' section."

"That wouldn't have made you look any taller."

"But there's always so much extra fabric I have to fold into the obi." Aoi groaned. "Could you help me with this?"

Sato grabbed a section of the yukata and tucked it into Aoi's fabric belt as he turned. He looked perfect for attending the summer festival.

Thankfully Aoi hadn't made a big deal about how their yukata matched, probably because Sato might've lied about that pattern being on sale. Aoi's was black with a geometric pattern of gray and white wheat-like stripes, while Sato's had the same pattern but in blue. Sato had figured if straight couples got to wear matching yukata to festivals, he and Aoi should be able to freely do the same.

Aoi grinned. "I can't tell if you're sexier in a yukata or a suit."

Sato leaned down to kiss Aoi, and Aoi's arms snaked around Sato and pulled him down to the awkward angle in which Aoi didn't need to stand on his toes.

Aoi tugged at Sato's collar then peeked inside. "Never mind. I like the yukata more. I get to see your nipples."

"Only if you pull down the collar." Sato grinned and pinched Aoi's ass. "I like you in a yukata more."

"Will you keep doing that if I wear them?"

"Maybe. You'll have to wear it again to see."

Aoi mock-frowned, and Sato pushed his glasses up to get Aoi's smile to return.

"Let's get going before all the games run out of prizes," Aoi said.

"They don't really run out of prizes."

"Oh." Aoi shrugged. "I was always stuck cooking behind a food stall during festivals, and we'd always end up running out of food. I figured the games worked the same way."

"You haven't played even one game?"

"That's why I got so excited when you asked if I wanted to go. So let's go. I want to win the best goldfish."

"You want a pet goldfish now?"

"It's not like we can handle anything else."

Aoi held Sato's hand and tugged him to the door. Of course, once they were outside the seclusion of their apartment, Aoi unlaced their fingers. Aoi had been so paranoid about people thinking they might be together, or perhaps it was because Sato no longer cared what anyone else thought anymore. The old ways were going away. People ate while walking down the street, and many young couples held hands and even kissed in public. If he wanted to squeeze Aoi's hand in public, they shouldn't have to worry about it.

Sato sighed as they got onto the train and sat next to each other. Sato was careful not to make their legs touch. He'd done it by accident a few days ago, and all of Aoi's muscles had tightened. Sure, it kind of made sense to be careful where they lived, but outside the anime district, Aoi was no one.

After a short ride, they got out and headed for the festival grounds.

The festival took up a good portion of the shrine grounds, and stalls were lined together with everything from food to games. The only break in the lines of booths was the stage in the center, where a woman and a man sang a duet onstage. About half of the people were dressed in yukata, and others in casual summer clothes, while the smell of fried food and the laughter of children lingered in the air.

Aoi's stomach grumbled.

"Should we get some food first, or you are still worried about getting the best goldfish?" Sato asked.

"Food first." Aoi clenched his hand into a fist and held it up. "Then with a full stomach, I'll be on my A-plus goldfish game."

Sato smiled. "Okay, let's get you fueled up for this winning streak. We'll have so many goldfish, we'll run out of names."

The food stalls were grouped toward the back of the festival so that everyone walked past the various games and vendors if they wanted anything to eat.

They stopped at a takoyaki stall and ordered a round of battered octopus for them both. Sato stuffed one of the balls in his mouth and held it open as he fanned his mouth due to the heat.

Aoi laughed. "At least you know how to eat them correctly now."

Sato took a step forward and kept his voice low. "How could I forget? That was the date that you kissed me."

"That was out of friendship."

"Uh-uh."

Aoi poked one of the balls with a toothpick. "You acted like you believed me."

"I might've for a little while."

Sato turned his head when he heard his name being called. He pushed up his glasses as his mom and dad came out of the crowd. They were the ones who'd told him about the festival, and Sato might've told them the times they'd be going.

Sato waved to his parents when Aoi wasn't looking, and they approached. Once they drew close, Aoi spotted them, but he didn't look as tense as he had during Sato's birthday. Maybe the monthly get-together of the four of them had finally paid off.

"Takoyaki is one of my favorites," Dad said.

Sato made a hole in one with this toothpick. "After the first one burns the roof of your mouth, the others are much easier to eat."

"How's the recording for the game going?" Mom asked.

She'd been trying to make a point to ask Aoi a few questions each time they met. Sato hoped Aoi could see how she was working to build a relationship between them, but anytime Sato had brought it up, Aoi always changed the subject.

"Okay." Aoi bit his lower lip. "We should be finished soon unless they need to rerecord something."

"How exciting! Congratulations."

Sato's mom clutched onto a pamphlet while she continued talking with Aoi. Then Sato saw the emblem on the paper in her hand: the unmistakable rainbow-colored clovers for the Association of LGBT Family and Friends. His parents had visited their booth long enough to grab a pamphlet?

Dad squeezed Mom's shoulder. "We should let them enjoy the festival. Let's make plans for next month sometime."

Sato smiled. "We'll do our best."

Aoi waved goodbye and stuffed the last of the takoyaki in his mouth. "Did you plan that?"

"They might've known we were coming."

"You could've warned me."

"But then you'd get all nervous. They chatted with us for like five minutes."

"Still." Aoi crumbled up his paper tray and tossed it in the bin. "Let's go play some games."

Even with his short legs, Aoi got ahead of Sato and found one of the many fishing booths. The dealer handed them both a rice-paper paddle and a bowl to place any fish he caught.

Sato placed his bowl in the shallow tank, and the fish darted anytime the bowl drew close. He tried to scoop up one of the fish, but it flopped against the wet paper, breaking it.

"Want to try again?" Aoi asked.

"I'll leave the pet-catching up to you."

Aoi hunched over the stall of water and skimmed the water with the paper paddle. "I read that you have to go slow to get one."

"You read up on goldfish scooping before we came?"

"No spreadsheets were involved."

"The spreadsheets make all the difference. If you made one, you'd have all the fish."

"Sshhh, you're going to scare all the fish."

Aoi stuck his tongue out and scooped up a fish then quickly slid it into the bowl.

"Lucky winner!" Sato cheered.

Aoi tried for a second, but the paper quickly broke. The stall owner gave Aoi a water bag.

"What should we name the fish?" Sato asked.

"Let's call him Gold."

"You can't call him Gold just because he's gold."

"Why not?"

"It would be like calling you Short and Cute."

Aoi pursed his lips.

"See?" Sato said. "Gold would be an offensive name. Let's call him Nightingale."

"So name the fish after a kind of bird?"

"Why not? It's a nice name."

Aoi sighed. "It's the name of a Gundam, isn't it?"

"A very pretty Gundam."

Aoi held up the fish. "Do you hear that, fish Nightingale? You're named after a pretty robot."

AUGUST

SATO JERKED AWAKE AT the *Gundam* opening theme song he'd set as his alarm on his phone. He yawned and turned it off. He curled his toes and stretched across the empty bed since Aoi had already gone on his morning run.

Maybe it would be good to surprise him by making breakfast. Sato had done it a few times before. Sure, the hard-boiled eggs had turned out runny, but he'd learned from the mistake.

But the bed was so cozy, and it was Saturday. He turned over, gathering up the corner of the blanket and burying his head in it. He could pretend to be asleep when Aoi returned and get a much more elaborate breakfast than toast and eggs. Sato buried his head in the blanket. Or Aoi might decide Sato wasn't eating healthily enough and he'd be stuck with cottage cheese and bananas.

He debated whether it was worth taking the chance, but then a knock on the door ended his debate. Aoi must've forgotten his keys again.

Sato got up. His mouth dropped as he opened the door to his mother.

She was dressed plainly but with a colorful pin on her blouse and a small wrapped gift in her hand.

"Mom, you came to visit?" Sato said.

She had never stepped foot inside their home.

"I won't stay long. Is Aoi around?"

"He's out for his run."

"Oh." She shuffled her feet.

"Why don't you come inside?"

Sato left the door open as he ducked into the sectioned-off bedroom area of the studio to put on some pants.

Mom chuckled. "This is exactly how I imagined your room would've turned out if we'd gotten you all the figures you wanted."

Sato stood beside one of the display cases filled with Gundam figures. "I only get a few a year, but over time, it builds up."

If twenty could be considered a few, then Sato wouldn't be lying. They had five display cases and rows of Aoi's boys'-love manga stacked in the space. They almost needed another bedroom for their obsessions.

"Is that the kotatsu table your father and I got you when you moved?" She sat at the low table.

Sato joined her. The small talk was odd for her, and the laugh lines around her eyes appeared deeper than usual.

"Is Dad okay?" Sato asked.

"Yes, everything's fine." She pushed the brown wrapped package forward. "This is for you and Aoi."

"You shouldn't have."

"Why don't you go ahead and open it while we wait for him."

Sato carefully unwrapped it, but then he noticed the pin his mother was wearing. It had rainbow-colored clovers with the words *Be Yourself* written in English. He pushed his glasses up to make sure he'd seen it right, and he had. His mother was wearing an LGBT-support pin. Had she worn it out in public where everyone could see or just pinned it on before she knocked on the door?

"They're yatsuhashi from our visit to Kyoto earlier this week," she said, getting Sato's attention. "They're very good. You should try one."

Sato opened the tin and pulled out one of the thin bridge-shaped cookies. The light cinnamon filled his nostrils before the cookie even made it to his tongue.

"You like them?" Mom asked.

Sato nodded. She grabbed one of cookies and ate it, then another one after the first was finished.

"Mom, is everything all right?" Sato asked.

She sighed and glanced at the door. "When does Aoi get back?"

"Usually not too much longer. Do you want to talk to him?"

She bit her lip, nodded, then grabbed another cookie. Sato leaned back and pushed up his glasses. He'd never seen his mom act so off before.

"What is it you want to talk to him about?"

"It's nothing bad. I just need to say something when you both are here."

Sato pressed his lips together. "I love Aoi with all my heart, Mom."

"I understand that now."

"It's good to hear."

She hugged her arms and stared at the table rather than meet her son's eyes.

"When your father and I visited the Shunkoin Temple, there was a wedding between two women."

"Oh?" Sato nodded and grabbed another cookie.

"Everyone looked so happy. And the brides were so beautiful. When they looked at each other, everyone could understand the love between them."

"It's nice when people find someone they want to be with for the rest of their lives."

She took in a deep breath. "Have you and Aoi talked about marriage?"

Sato coughed. "Excuse me?"

"You guys have dated longer than your father and I dated before we were married."

"We haven't really talked about it, and it's not exactly legal everywhere." Sato rubbed his neck.

"But if it was? Would Aoi be the one?"

Sato's heart thumped in his chest, and he opened his mouth but then closed it. "I—we—"

The door opened.

"I'm home," Aoi called out. He did a double take at Sato's mom and gave a formal bow. "It's a surprise to see you here, Mrs. Emi."

"It's nice to see you again." She stood and returned Aoi's bow.

"I should go take a shower."

"Could you please wait for a few minutes before? I think if I have to wait any longer to say it, I'll grow a dress size eating because of my nerves."

Aoi glanced toward Sato, who shrugged.

"A few months ago, my husband suggested we join the Association of LGBT Family and Friends. I wasn't sure at first, but I joined because of Sato. It hasn't been too long, but going to their meetings and listening to the people speak, I've realized I've said and done things that have hurt you. I'm sorry for what I've said, and know that I must show you with my actions, not my words, to earn your forgiveness."

Aoi's face reddened, but he smiled. "Thank you."

She turned to Sato. "And I'm sorry you felt like you had to hide who you were from us all those years. I hope you never have to feel that way again."

Sato smiled. "Thanks, Mom. I know it's been hard for you, but I'm glad you see there was nothing to worry about."

She nodded and glanced back at Aoi. "Sato said you don't get along well with your parents, but I wanted to tell you as long as you are with Sato, I'll consider you another son."

"Thank you."

"I wish you both a wonderful morning. Don't be shy about coming over."

"We won't," Sato said.

She left, and once the door closed, Aoi sank to his knees. A sharp inhalation of breath came and then the tears. Sato ran over and wrapped Aoi in a hug, but he knew they were tears of joy.

SEPTEMBER

AOI RAN HIS FINGERS through his hair, but the amount of hair spray on his blond locks left his fingers trapped in the stiff side wave.

"Try not to mess with it, or we'll have to redo it," the hair-and-makeup stylist said.

"Sorry."

"First time on TV?"

"Yeah."

She dabbed some powder on Aoi's face. "Everyone gets nervous the first time."

The fact the interview was being televised wasn't what was making Aoi's stomach twist up like soba noodles; it was the fact it was *another* interview with Atsushi. Sure, he and Atsushi were the bigger names on the hit dating-sim game, but did they really have to do every interview together?

Each interview, Atsushi got a little bolder. At first, he'd do a little typical teasing, poking fun at Aoi's height, but then the offhand comments came closer and closer to Aoi's personal life. His stomach twisted a little more as he thought about what the interview would've been like if two of the other actors hadn't joined them.

The woman took a step back and examined Aoi's face. "Try to focus not on the camera, but the audience behind it. Don't worry. Boz and Mei are amazing and will get everyone laughing."

Aoi smiled. "Thanks."

She tickled Aoi's nose with the makeup brush one last time. "All done. Next!"

Atsushi walked in, blowing an air-kiss at Aoi before plopping in the chair. He had the stylist giggling like a schoolgirl in seconds.

Aoi fled the room and stood behind the side curtain with the other voice actors. The afternoon TV show focused on geek culture and featured anything from video games to the latest street fashion. Aoi had never seen the show before, but Sato had mentioned he'd sometimes watched it when they'd interviewed *Gundam* people.

Mei and Boz walked onto the set. Mei began a funny story about going shopping over the weekend to warm up the audience. She wore a frilly gothic-princess–looking dress with a crown made out of black and red roses.

The other host, Boz, had greeted Aoi before he'd gone into makeup. Boz's thin-rimmed glasses reminded him of Sato, but the bright pattern on his shirt gave off more of a cool-video-game-nerd vibe than Sato would've ever been able to pull off.

They gave a little background on the dating-simulation game and then brought all the cast on set. There was more joking and laughter, and any nerves about being stuck with Atsushi vanished. There were six of them to defuse anything Atsushi might want to say.

"With so many of them, I think we should bring out the wheel and see what game to play with these guys," Mei said.

The audience cheered as a large spinning wheel was brought on set.

Aoi's eyes grew wide. They were all thinly veiled kissing games.

"Let's spin the wheel," Boz said to cheer on the audience.

Mei stood and spun the wheel while the audience clapped. It turned and turned, and each one held Aoi's fate until it slowed to a stop on the Pocky game. Out of all of the games, it was the one meant to make them kiss the most.

"How do they play this?" Boz asked, tapping the Pocky box containing the chocolate-covered biscuit.

"Each player will put one end of the Pocky in his mouth and eat until they are in the middle. The first to pull away loses. If their lips touch, it's a tie."

Aoi scooted a little closer to Hiro. Atsushi was the last person Aoi wanted to play the game with, and Hiro would be nice enough not to full-on kiss him because he could. The move made the audience chuckle.

"I see Aoi already picked his partner," Boz said.

"The winner of the matches will go on and play each other to see who will be to be the ultimate victor," Mai said.

Aoi grabbed the stick cookie offered to him and sighed as he turned toward Hiro. He looked just as excited as Aoi was about the whole situation. It didn't matter really because Aoi had it all planned out; after the second bite of the cookie, Aoi would pull away so he wouldn't have to go against Atsushi.

"Ready? Go!" Mei said.

Hiro put the other end of the Pocky stick in his mouth, and a second after Mei called, "Go!" Hiro laughed. He didn't even get one bite in before being called out. Aoi glared at him, but all Hiro did was laugh, his whole face turning red. The audience *aww*ed in disappointment.

Of course Atsushi won.

Aoi's insides twisted. The audience cheered, and another Pocky stick was handed to him.

Aoi sighed.

The cheering grew louder as Atsushi sat in the seat beside Aoi.

"I'm ready for this." Atsushi rubbed his hands together.

Aoi bit the inside of his cheek and hoped the death glare he shot Atsushi wasn't obvious. Though the way the jackass grinned, he knew exactly what Aoi thought of the game.

Aoi couldn't pull away like Hiro had, or else the audience would be mad again, but he couldn't allow Atsushi to kiss him.

He put the cookie in his mouth, and Atsushi followed, taking the first large bite.

Aoi followed with a smaller one.

Then Atsushi went in for the second bite, and more than half of the stick was gone. In two more bites, their lips would touch. Aoi grinned as best he could around the cookie and then pulled the rest of the treat into his mouth.

The audience laughed.

Atsushi stared at him blankly then leaned forward and kissed him anyway. Aoi shoved him away, and the audience exploded in laughter and cheers at the assault. Even the hosts were laughing at his expense. His insides burned, and he bit the inside of his cheek to keep himself from screaming.

Eventually, everyone settled down, and the interview ended with Aoi squeaking out responses only when absolutely necessary. As soon as the host called the show to an end, Aoi got up and left.

"Aoi! Aoi!" Atsushi chased after him.

Aoi tried to ignore all the racing thoughts.

"Where you going?" Atsushi called.

Aoi turned and stared at Atsushi. "You touch me again, and I don't care if you're on national TV—I'm going to beat the shit out of you."

He brushed past Atsushi, not giving him time to respond. Aoi had enough to deal with, like how he was going to explain the kiss to Sato.

SEPTEMBER BONUS

AOI HAD NEVER FELT threatened by a door in his life, but standing outside his apartment, it loomed over him worse than any claustrophobic nightmare.

Sato waited for him on the other side. His smile would spread across his face the second Aoi stepped over the threshold, but it wouldn't last. The second Sato watched the interview, there would be no more smiles.

The lump in Aoi's throat proved impossible to swallow, and the slow thump of his heart made his whole body ache. He was a better person because of Sato, and the shitfaced Atsushi had gone and ruined it.

Aoi sighed.

If Sato weren't so supportive of everything Aoi did, then he wouldn't have to worry about it. Aoi would have to go in there sometime, and it would be better if Sato saw what had happened with him there to explain it rather than not. Aoi fished the keys out of his pocket and opened the door.

"I'm home," Aoi called out.

"Welcome home."

"How was work?"

"The usual. I have everything set up to watch your first TV interview with you. You can tell me all the behind-the-scenes details."

Aoi wrapped his arms around Sato's waist then stood on his tiptoes, and instinctually Sato leaned down to meet Aoi's lips. They were the only lips he ever wanted to kiss.

Aoi snaked his hand underneath Sato's shirt. A small moan released from the back of Sato's throat and urged Aoi on. He could seduce Sato and drive him to such sweet release he'd forget all about the interview. Aoi's fingers tickled up Sato's ribs then pinched at his nipple.

Sato gasped and nipped at Aoi's neck before cupping Aoi's hand still.

"I've been wanting to see it all day," Sato said. "Let's watch the interview before we get too carried away."

Aoi grinned. "The interview can wait—let's celebrate."

"But it was the first time you were on TV."

"It wasn't like I was by myself."

"It was national TV."

Aoi crossed his arms. "Atsushi was there."

"I know you hate him, but it was live TV. He couldn't have been a jerk on camera."

"He was."

Sato pushed up his glasses. "It's only what? Ten minutes? We can watch it, and then I can help you forget all about Atsushi."

Aoi sighed. "I'm telling you he was horrible."

"Don't let him ruin your first TV appearance."

"Fine. We can watch it."

Sato would eventually see it, and it was probably best to get it over with. They lay in bed with the laptop resting between them.

"This isn't too bad. You're doing good."

Aoi closed his eyes and let the voices wash over him.

"Did you know about the game before?" Sato asked.

"They just said there were going to be games. I figured it would be some kind of drawing thing or writing out words in English. They usually do stuff like that."

"So when it landed on the Pocky game?"

"I had no idea. I tried to lose, but then Hiro kept on laughing, and I won. Then Atsushi…"

Aoi closed his eyes tighter as the audience laughed then cheered.

"He actually kissed you?" Sato said. "Couldn't you have done something about it?"

"I shoved him away."

"I know, but I mean—"

"I called my agent and made sure there wouldn't be something like that again, but that was all I could really do. Backstage, he gloated about how it would boost my career and I should thank him."

"But that's not right. You didn't agree to it in the first place."

"If I make a bigger deal about it, Atsushi will hold over the fact I'm gay as blackmail. He keeps on talking about how I should come out all the time."

Sato bit his lip. "Well, maybe you should and he'll stop harassing you."

"Sato!"

"Maybe he'll stop after you do it."

"And it will be the end of my career."

"You play gay characters. You think all of your fans are huge hypocrites?"

"They're not the ones who hire me. The producers and the directors are."

Sato sighed. "And they'd want popular people to fill the roles. Your fans would love you any way you are. If you don't believe me, then ask Michiko."

"You know who else I thought would love me no matter what?" Aoi crossed his arms. "My parents. And you know how that ended."

"It's not the same."

"I can't believe you're taking Atsushi's side!"

Aoi ran his fingers through his hair, still sticky from all the hair spray. It was like he cheated on Sato, and it was all Atsushi's fault for everything.

"I'm not taking his side," Sato said.

"You're so taking his side. Maybe you're okay coming out with a rainbow parade, but I'm not."

"I don't mean it like that."

Aoi balled his hand into a fist around the bedsheet. "You've been pushing me for months. First with the monthly outings with your family—"

"That's because I want you to be more comfortable around them. Is that wrong?"

"No." Aoi sighed. "It's just too much for me. I have another interview with him tomorrow too. I don't want to do it."

"Can you cancel? Pretend you're sick or something?"

"No, if I call in sick, it looks bad, and then it's almost like Atsushi won. I just need a drink."

"We have some beer in the fridge."

Aoi shook his head. "I want to go out."

"Oh, well—"

"I'll be back late, so don't stay up."

"Aoi…"

Aoi walked out the door.

THERE WAS ONLY ONE person Aoi could go drinking with—Jin—and thankfully the rock-star vocalist wasn't on tour.

Aoi knocked on his door, and after a few minutes he answered the door shirtless. His long blond hair stuck up in every direction, and his black jeans weren't even buttoned.

Aoi raised an eyebrow. "Did I get you at a bad time?"

Jin kept hold of the door, and he leaned against the frame. "No, everything's good. Did you and Sato get in a fight?"

"What makes you think that?"

"Why else would you come here unannounced?"

A black pug squeezed between Jin's legs and trotted down the hallway.

"Princess Potato, get back here!" Jin called.

Her little legs ran faster.

Jin groaned and chased after the dog as she ran down the stairs. The door widened on its own, and Aoi peeked inside Jin's apartment to find a guy inside, pulling up his pants. His blue hair meant he could've been anyone from the music scene, but then he turned, and Aoi could have recognized that pierced face anywhere.

"Kazuki?" Aoi said. "I thought you liked women."

He zipped himself up and shrugged. "I like men too."

Aoi laughed. "Oh man, you guys are a thing now?"

"Maybe. I don't…" He gnawed at one of his four lip piercings. "We haven't really talked about it with the rest of the band yet."

Kazuki was the leader of Lilith, and Aoi knew band politics would dictate whether Jin and Kazuki could be anything more than a casual hookup, even if they both wanted more. Though for as long as Aoi had known Jin, he'd lusted after the band's straight drummer.

Aoi shrugged. "Has to be something if you convinced Jin to see you and you're bi. He swore he'd never date someone who also liked women."

Jin's scolding of the Princess about getting out of her palace preceded him as he climbed the stairs. He held the chubby pug in his arms, and she licked his fingers.

"We're not dating," Jin said.

"Like how Sato and I were *just friends*," Aoi said.

"Did something happen between you two?" Kazuki asked.

Aoi swallowed. "Bad day. You guys up for going drinking, or should I let you get back to what you were doing?"

"It'll be like old times."

"And I won't have to worry about making sure you guys aren't hungover enough to perform."

Kazuki laughed. "Those were some wild times when we were still indie."

"I'm up for it," Jin said. "Let me get my shirt on."

"Maybe we can go to a bar where the shirts are optional." Kazuki licked over one of his lip piercings.

"Aoi doesn't want to go to any of your kinky BDSM clubs."

Jin grabbed a tight black shirt with shiny silver writing on it. Then Jin took Aoi's wrist.

"Tell us what happened, and then we can get you so wasted you can forget all about it."

The train ride to the gay club Aoi and Jin used to haunt was filled with Aoi telling every jerkface thing Atsushi had done, from locking him in a room and making him late for Sato and Aoi's first Christmas to the kissing on live TV.

The bar was an old haunt where Jin used to bartend. It could only fit twenty people, but the bright paint and mix of rock and pop songs from different decades put them right at home.

They sat at the bar and ordered a round of drinks.

"Don't worry. You know we can keep up with you and help you forget about it," Jin said.

His tone was sincere, but he hadn't looked up from his phone for the past few minutes.

Aoi leaned over and glanced at Jin's phone. "You're playing the dating sim after everything I said!"

"It's not my fault that it's a good game."

Aoi crossed his arms. "Well, at least don't get my character with Atsushi's."

Jin laughed. "Okay, okay."

"I'm not downloading it," Kazuki said.

"See, that's why you're the band leader."

"Can't you voice-act in non-BL stuff? Then you wouldn't have to worry about Atsushi so much."

Aoi bit his lip. "But I like doing BL scripts."

"Sometimes we have to put out singles that are more pop so we can put get fans interested in the hard-rock stuff."

"It would feel like I'm starting over from scratch. I wouldn't know what to do."

Jin squeezed Aoi's shoulder. "You're good. It'll come naturally."

The first round of drinks was delivered, and Aoi rubbed his finger along the glass of the neon-blue concoction. Maybe Kazuki and Jin were right. Aoi couldn't play the submissive in boys'-love gigs all the time. What was he going to do when he got older?

"To old times!" Aoi held up his glass.

They clinked them together, and Aoi finished his first drink, slammed the glass on the counter, and called for another.

EVEN WITH SATO NIPPING at Aoi's ear, the sweet gesture only made the ringing louder in his head. At least whatever had happened last night killed any thoughts of the interview today, since the only thing Aoi could focus on were the bells in his head.

"I made you breakfast," Sato said.

Aoi rubbed his face. "Does it include more alcohol?"

"Don't you think that's the last thing you need?"

Aoi turned over and tried to look at Sato, but the sun blazed in the window. He closed his eyes and groaned.

"No. I have that interview with a jackass in a few hours. Alcohol seems perfect," Aoi mumbled.

"Well, you get pain meds and toast. Come on. Time to get up."

Sato offered Aoi a glass of water in one hand and the pills in the other. Aoi took them and hoped they'd work by the time he headed out for the interview. Aoi couldn't wait to go back to rereading script lines and moaning all day. If the game died today, it wouldn't be soon enough.

Sato pushed up his glasses. "Must've been a good night for you to pass on your morning run."

"Shit. Sorry. Did the alarm wake you up?"

"It's okay. I tried waking you up, but you mumbled something and went back to sleep. Figured you could use it."

Aoi squeezed Sato's hand and grabbed the toast from the plate beside him with his other hand. Sato made everything better. Too bad he couldn't take him onstage during the interview, but at least he'd be there in the audience.

"Where did you go last night?" Sato asked.

Aoi munched on a bit of toast. "Went to see Jin and met up with Kazuki. We all went drinking at one of the old bars he used to work at, but after that, it's kind of a blur."

"You shouldn't drink so much."

"I know." Aoi rubbed an eye with the back of his palm. "But I wanted to forget about Atsushi."

Sato looked off at one of his display shelves.

"Did I do something?" Aoi asked.

Sato sighed. "Not that Atsushi's right, but if you did come out, he wouldn't have anything to hang over your head."

Aoi took a loud bite of his toast. "We talked about this last night."

"No, we didn't. I mentioned it, then you ran out."

"If I came out, it would ruin my career."

"Any of your true fans would be happy you were being honest with them."

"Too bad it's the directors and producers who hire me."

"You voice-act gay characters. How can they not want you? I don't know how many different ways I can say it."

"Then why don't you put homosexual on your resume?"

Sato rubbed his temple. "Your true fans would flock to the projects you worked on."

"I'd get one gig a year. If that."

"So what? You won't have to stress if you're never stuck with a project with Atsushi."

Sato reached out and squeezed Aoi's hand. He wanted to pull away, but he knew it was right. Sato knew him better than he knew himself.

Aoi shook his head.

"I know you worry about money, but we'll be fine," Sato said. "You made two phenomenal hits, and we went over the investments we made. We can live off the profits between gigs. If anything, I can take up a few freelance jobs if we need it. And it's not like I have to buy every robot that comes out."

Aoi sighed. Sato shouldn't have to take on extra work because Aoi fucked up his career by coming out.

"What do you think?" Sato asked.

"I'll think about it. Thanks again for making breakfast."

"I know it's not as good as when you make it."

Aoi smiled. "You'll get there one day. Did you make any coffee with it?"

"I'll go make us a pot."

"Thanks."

Aoi finished off the toast and grabbed his blinking phone. His eyes narrowed. At least a hundred notifications had popped up during the night on his various social media apps. Atsushi must've posted something scandalous and tagged Aoi on it.

He clicked on the app with the largest numbers and scrolled through until he got to the original source of all the motivation.

It was a video.

And one he'd uploaded.

Shit.

The ringing in his head grew louder as he clicked to play the video. Through the shaky movements, he saw the bar he'd gone drinking at with Jin and Kazuki.

Everyone at the bar was singing along to a decade-old pop song, and then the video panned to the bar top. Jin lay across it with his shirt pulled up to his neck. The bartender placed a Jell-O shot on Jin's stomach. It jiggled with his giggles.

Then what got all the hits finally happened. Aoi had bent down and eaten the shot off Jin's stomach. The bar cheered as Aoi came up, and the video ended.

Aoi sighed.

His drunk ass had actually fucking uploaded it to all his media channels. If he deleted it, then it would just get worse.

He sank back into the bed and curled into a ball. He shut his eyes, but the image of him licking Jell-O off Jin's stomach stayed. Aoi had to tell Sato about it. Granted, he kept to *Gundam* forums and would probably never see it.

The bed shifted under Sato's weight.

"I don't think hiding under the covers will stop the interview from happening," Sato said. "The coffee's ready."

Aoi clutched onto the blanket but knew it had to be done. He grabbed his mug of coffee and swallowed a gulp down. It burned his throat, but Aoi deserved the punishment.

"I don't really remember last night, but there's something you should see."

Aoi twisted the blanket between his fingers but still handed the phone to Sato. Aoi looked away, but the audio was impossible to escape. He could replay the video a hundred times in his head, and in each version, Sato's imagined reaction grew more bombastic—all the things Sato would yell at him about before slamming the door in his face.

The video sound had stopped, but Sato said nothing. Aoi had no idea how long the seconds ticked by, but when he'd finally built up enough courage to look at Sato, his lover's frown made Aoi hate himself a little more.

"I know you've been with a lot of guys before me, so maybe this isn't a big deal to you, but it is to me," Sato said.

"It was stupid. I shouldn't have drunk so much."

"That's the understatement of the century."

Aoi's bottom lip trembled. "I'm sorry."

Sato's shoulders dropped, and he looked away. His silence stung worse than anything Aoi could have imagined. Like a thousand tiny papercuts slicing though his skin at once. Sato had every right to be angry and every right to leave Aoi right then.

"Masatomo." Aoi somehow managed to squeak out Sato's first name. "Please, I—"

"It's not like you took a shot off his dick." Sato sighed and squeezed Aoi's hand. "But I should be the only person you take Jell-O shots off of."

"I know."

"Good. I'm glad we're *now* on the same page." Sato's voice was firm.

Aoi leaned in to kiss Sato, but he jerked away, his chin held high.

"I forgive you, but I still have every right to be mad right now."

"Oh."

Aoi glanced back at the goldfish on the nightstand on his side. Somehow Nightingale had managed to survive the past three months. Aoi rubbed his eyes. They'd been so happy at the festival, and Aoi'd had to go fuck it all up.

He took in a deep breath. Sato's mom had gone from crying and running into the other room then to joining an LGBT group. Maybe everyone wasn't like Aoi's parents.

"Shouldn't you leave for your interview?" Sato asked.

"Yeah, they want me there early so Atsushi can take a few punches before getting me on set."

Sato rolled his eyes. "He's feeding off how worked up you get."

"The guy kissed me."

"You and I both know that was meaningless fan service." Sato shook his head. "You need to figure out how to deal with Atsushi, or else we're going to keep on having the same talk every time you work with him."

Sato was right, but Aoi didn't want to admit it. Aoi stood and walked away, but Sato grabbed his hand.

"You'll do amazing." Sato's smile looked forced, but he gave Aoi's hand a squeeze, the meaning Aoi could never doubt.

"Thanks. I'll see you later."

AOI UNDERSTOOD THE HURRY-UP-AND-WAIT with TV production more with each experience. He had to arrive hours before the interview and wait hours for his turn for hair and makeup even though it took less than thirty minutes once he actually sat in the chair. After that, he was nothing more than a body sitting in a room with the production staff checking that he hadn't wandered off every few minutes.

He leaned over the arm of the sofa and stared at his phone. He'd imagined Sato would've contacted him about something.

But no.

He was probably still pissed off. He had every right to be.

Aoi tapped on his phone. He'd wanted to text Sato about how Atsushi had been so full of himself he'd nearly slammed Aoi against the wall when he brushed passed him into makeup. He and Sato always had the same back-and-forth when it came to Atsushi. Aoi couldn't let Atsushi sour his relationship with Sato like that. He couldn't imagine being with anyone else, and he was the one driving the wedge between them with all Atsushi's talk of coming out.

Atsushi had said when he'd come out as bisexual, it had boosted his career. Aoi poked at his phone, searching for the interview where he'd mentioned it.

After a few minutes of searching, Aoi found the page. The interview had been years ago, and his coming out had been more of an offhand comment about how he liked girls but sometimes thought some guys were cute. But comparing it to the jobs he'd been getting, Aoi saw that he'd gotten a little bump after the interview before slumping back to his usual.

A stagehand knocked on the door. "Aoi, you're up in five."

Aoi slid the phone back into his pocket and followed her. The phone burned against his skin. If nothing bad had happened to Atsushi when he'd come out, why would it be any different for Aoi?

The female host welcomed Aoi on set. She introduced the dating-sim game and talked about how even she'd become addicted to it. All the questions were easy, and thankfully she didn't bring up the video from last night.

"Is there anything you want to say before we bring out one of your costars?" she asked.

Aoi pressed his lips together. Everyone in the audience stared at him, as if they already knew what he was going to say and judged him for it.

He opened his mouth, but the memory of the day he'd come home as a teen to find a trash bag filled with his clothes waiting outside for him burned his throat and choked his words. Aoi tried to push back the memory of his parents kicking him out, but it only grew.

He couldn't confess who he really was to them. They all wouldn't understand. They wouldn't bother to listen. Their hate would spread, and he wouldn't be able to find another job again, and it would mean both he and Sato would be on the streets.

Then a familiar face smiled at him from the back of the audience. It was Sato. Sure, Aoi had given him a ticket, but it had been before the fight and the Jell-O shot.

Sato's smile grew wider as their gazes met, and it was all the strength Aoi needed. He had to come out for both of them.

"Actually, I've wanted to say something for a few months now, but now feels like the best time." Aoi cleared his throat and kept his focus on Sato.

"Well, now you have my attention," the hostess said.

The audience laughed, and Aoi continued. "I wanted to say sometimes I'm able to really connect with the characters I play because I'm gay too. I hope my fans will be happy that I can finally be who I am with them."

Sato took off his glasses and rubbed his eyes before he joined in the audience applause. It took all of Aoi's strength not run up and hug him.

Aoi leaned back in his chair, and for the first time, he could breathe. The hostess congratulated Aoi then called Atsushi. The smug look on his face had disappeared.

"I'm so glad this guy finally came out." He leaned forward and ruffled Aoi's hair. "I've been trying to convince him for ages. When I came out as bi, it was the best feeling."

"Really?" The hostess raised an eyebrow. "I never knew. You two could be the next power anime couple."

Aoi shook his head. The last thing there needed to be was more fan fiction of him and Atsushi together.

"I already have someone special," Aoi said.

"Oh? Can you tell us more?"

"Just that he's very special to me. Everything else is a secret."

The interview continued without a hitch. Atsushi was less irritating—Aoi hadn't thought that was possible.

Once it ended, Aoi headed backstage to find Sato waiting for him. Aoi's heart fluttered in his chest. For once, they didn't have to wait until hours after an event to see each other and then look both ways to make sure no one else was there.

"They let me backstage since I was your guest. This is so cool," Sato said, looking around.

"When I saw you in the audience, I was shocked."

"I was only a little mad at you, and there was no way I was going to miss seeing you being interviewed on TV."

"Thanks."

Sato pushed up his glasses and took a step closer to Aoi. "I'm shocked you came out."

Aoi's cheeks burned. "I did it for both of us."

"I hope you did it mostly for yourself, though."

Aoi smiled and nodded. "Yeah."

He stood on his toes and gave Sato a kiss. Aoi no longer cared if anyone saw them. Whatever happened to his career, he knew Sato would be by his side, and together they had the strength to do anything.

Sato squeezed Aoi's hand. "Let's go home."

"Okay. I'll make Jell-O."

Sato laughed. "Sounds like fun."

AUTHOR NOTE

H I EVERYONE!

Thank you for picking up *Year Two*. This marks my second year of newsletter stories featuring Aoi and Sato. I let my inner high school fangirl out with these guys and put in all my favorite tropes from Japanese manga. If you enjoyed the book please leave a review. It helps more people discover Aoi and Sato and gets me one step closer to my dream of becoming a full-time author. If you want more Aoi and Sato now don't forget to subscribe to the newsletter. You'll get a new short story the first of every month. Thanks again for your continued support. I would be nothing without my readers.

thank you,
Amy
September 1, 2018

ABOUT THE AUTHOR

AMY TASUKADA LIVES IN North Texas with a calico cat called O'Hara. As an only child her day dreams kept her entertained, and at age ten she started to put them to paper. Since then her love of writing hasn't cease. She can be found drinking hot tea and filming Japanese street fashion hauls on her Youtube channel.

Connect with Amy on…

WEBSITE:
www.amytasukada.com

FACEBOOK:
facebook.com/amytasukadaofficial

TWITTER:
twitter.com/amytasukada

YOUTUBE:
www.youtube.com/user/amytasukada

www.ingramcontent.com/pod-product-compliance
Lightning Source LLC
Chambersburg PA
CBHW032034180726
48284CB00008B/2582